Love Comes in Small Packages

BOOKS BY LORI FOSTER

The Guest Cottage

Too Much Temptation

Never Too Much

Unexpected

Say No to Joe?

The Secret Life of Bryan

When Bruce Met Cyn

Just a Hint—Clint

Jamie

Murphy's Law

Jude's Law

ANTHOLOGIES

In Bloom

The Two of Us

The Watson Brothers

Yule Be Mine

Give It Up

BOOKS BY MAISEY YATES

Lonesome Ridge

Rustler Mountain

Outlaw Lake

ANTHOLOGIES

Santa's on His Way

The Two of Us

Small Town Hero

Love Comes in Small Packages

LORI FOSTER

MAISEY YATES

kensingtonbooks.com

KENSINGTON BOOKS are published by

Kensington Publishing Corp.
900 Third Avenue
New York, NY 10022

ISBN: 978-1-4967-5417-2
ISBN: 978-1-4967-5418-9 (ebook)

First Kensington Trade Paperback Printing: April 2026

10 9 8 7 6 5 4 3 2 1

Printed in the United States of America

The authorized representative in the EU for product safety and compliance
is eucomply OU, Parnu mnt 139b-14, Apt 123
Tallinn, Berlin 11317, hello@eucompliancepartner.com

CONTENTS

That Special Someone

LORI FOSTER

Special thanks to my Facebook followers, who always help out when I need a name—for a human or a pet.

When I asked on my page, reader Danielle Walther offered up the name "River" for a cat. It turned into the *perfect* name—especially for a cat that liked to steal the show.

CHAPTER 1

Of course it was in the low nineties in early September. The broiling sun hung like a fiery ball in the cloudless afternoon sky. Ohio weather was always unpredictable, but usually by now the temps would be mid to high seventies.

No one wanted to shingle a roof in this heat, but after a destructive rainstorm, and with more rain in the forecast, it was now or never for the elderly customers who'd hired him. No way could he leave them with a leaking roof.

Thankfully, Knox Nial had a great crew. They weren't complaining, so he couldn't complain. Good thing they'd started early and the house was small.

He had his hammer raised when the phone in his back pocket buzzed. Pausing, he fished it out to glance at the screen. His friend Ford had recently married and was finally able to take his wife on a brief getaway. Knox had volunteered to pet sit their two dogs—with the help of Ford's new sister-in-law, which Knox considered a bonus.

It was the sister-in-law, Laylee Fairchild, calling him now. She knew he was roofing today, which made him worry there might be a problem with one of the dogs. He answered on the third ring. "What's up? Everything okay?"

He didn't realize he'd accidentally put her on speaker until she loudly wailed, "Knox, I think I'm pregnant!"

Several things happened at once.

The other three men went silent. Knox fumbled the phone, tried to grab it, and lost his footing. Both he and the phone tumbled right over the side of the roof, landing in ancient shrubbery.

For several seconds, Knox didn't move. He was half in, half out of the bushes, which—maybe—had broken his fall. The other men were shouting, quickly descending the ladder, and he finally got it together enough to groan.

Laylee was still talking a mile a minute, so he grabbed for the phone, getting more scratches in the process, and said, "Give me just a sec."

There was a brief hesitation, and she asked, "Why do you sound like that?" And then, with a touch of anger, "You aren't the dad, Knox! We haven't even had sex."

The guys, who had been in the process of reaching for him, all grinned.

Knox said, "I fell off the roof."

"You . . . *what?*"

"I'm fine." He hoped. Accepting a hand, he scrambled to his feet, checked his body, and decided other than bloody scratches and a few likely bruises, he'd survived. "Hold on." He held the phone against his thigh and drew a breath.

Pregnant. Okay, he hadn't seen that one coming.

When he thought of Laylee, as he often did, it was the two of them together—which, admittedly, hadn't happened yet, but he was working on it. Some other dude in the picture, though? Damn.

He glanced at the guys, saw them all waiting, and frowned. "I need to take this call."

The three of them nodded.

Willie, the oldest at forty-seven, who'd started with Knox's dad before Knox had taken over the construction company, gave a snort. "You shouldn't keep her waiting. She sounded upset." Nothing much bothered Willie, so he headed back up the ladder, calling over his shoulder, "You two. Get back to work."

The two younger men lingered because they were snoops. Knox knew they'd be ribbing him for weeks about this. Pointing to his Silverado, which was parked on the street, he said, "I'm going to sit in the truck for privacy." Not for the air-conditioning, though he wouldn't complain about that part. "You heard Willie. Back to work."

As he walked away, he took the phone off speaker and put it to his ear. "Laylee?"

She screeched, "*You fell off a roof?*"

Wincing, he opened his truck door. A miserable blast of heat poured out. "Yeah." He started the engine and turned the air on full blast. "But I'm fine."

"Oh, my God, Knox, I'm so sorry. It's my fault, isn't it? I startled you."

Startled him? She'd damn near stopped his heart. "Don't worry about me. You said you're pregnant?"

He heard two deep breaths, and then she whispered, "I think I might be."

Which meant she also might *not* be. "Okay, one step at a time. Tell me why you think that."

"Please know that I wouldn't bother you with this, except Skye is away with Ford, and the last thing I want to do is bother her. Oh, Knox, she's so happy right now."

"So is Ford." He smiled, and now that the truck had cooled, he closed the door and sat back. "I take it you need someone to talk to?" Count him in. Hell, even if there was a bun in the oven, he was still interested. He liked kids. He more than liked Laylee and had from the first moment he'd seen her. For months now, they'd been getting to know each other better.

His very first glimpse of her had snagged him because the woman was incredibly beautiful. Model-worthy, and in fact she did do local modeling and seemed successful. Plenty of reason for an insta-attraction there.

But at twenty-five, he'd known his fair share of attractive women. It was everything else about Laylee that made him think in terms of a relationship—her love for her sister, her boldness mixed with her occasional uncertainty, and the easy way she'd fit in with his group of close friends.

"They're perfect for each other," she said. "And yes, I bought a pregnancy test but now I'm afraid to do it."

Alone. She was afraid to do it alone, and that's where he could step in. "So how about I finish up here and head your way? We'll do it together."

She choked.

"I don't plan to pee on the thing," he teased. "I just meant I'd be there with you."

Her voice softened, losing its edge. "You know how to do a pregnancy test, Knox?"

"I have a little sis, so yeah, I know." Then he thought to add, "She's two years younger and wants a family, just not yet. It was negative, by the way."

"I didn't know you had a sister."

They were getting off topic, but she was definitely calmer now, so he didn't mind. "Sis recently turned twenty-four and my brother is now twenty-one. You'll like them. You'll like Mom and Dad, too."

There was a long pause before she asked, "I'll be meeting them?"

"Whenever you want." He looked forward to introducing her to his family.

Laylee cleared her throat. "Okay, cool. I'd like that. Anytime is fine by me."

"We'll figure it out. But for now, how about that test? You want to wait for me?"

"You're working. I mean, I knew that, but I'd forgotten when I called. I got home with the test kit, took it out of the bag, and then a wave of panic hit me. I might have freaked out Maybelline and Tank."

The two dogs, both rescued from a shelter, were closely bonded yet as different as night from day. Maybelline was enormous, and whether Ford wanted to admit it or not, she was pretty damned homely. Sweet as could be, sure, but not a pretty sight. Tank was an itty-bitty thing who lacked Maybelline's gentle nature. He was a feisty one, always ready to rumble, but once you won him over, he could be a sweetheart.

"The dogs will be fine," he assured Laylee. "They feel secure now and they know they're loved. They can handle you getting a little stressed."

"Stressed and terrified."

Yeah, he could hear the anxiety in her voice. "So, does the guy know you might be—"

"God, no. It was just a . . . desperate quickie?" She made a disgusted sound. "He wasn't even that attractive, Knox! What was I thinking?" On a roll, she sneered, "But oh, I was feeling sorry for myself—a bad habit, for real—and he was a mistake that happened. I mean, not that he was icky or anything. I do have some standards."

"I understand." If only she'd come to him instead. "You only saw him once?" Not that he wanted details, God no, but if she was still involved with the guy, it mattered.

"One and done," she promised. "Anyway, it dawned on me that things were . . . off. Then I wondered why and the big pregnancy scare hit. I want to be sure before I even think of talking to a guy."

Damn it, *he* was a guy. Or hadn't she even noticed? "Good decision." If Knox had anything to say about it—not that he did yet, obviously—all other guys could take a hike. "We'll work it out, okay?"

"Knox," she breathed softly. "You're the best friend a girl ever had."

He barely kept his groan contained. Stuck in the friend zone.

Hell, it was better than being shut out completely, but it wasn't even close to where he wanted to be.

"No need to cut your day short," she said. "Just telling someone else helped."

"Sure, but you told *me*, right? Not just anyone, so why not wait until I'm with you?" Then, if it wasn't the news she wanted, or even if it was, he'd be there for her.

"Thank you, I will. I meant that you don't have to rush. You can finish up your day."

"What will you do?"

"Wait for you."

That sounded nice. "You promise?"

"You were planning to come by anyway, right? So we could walk the dogs?"

It was as good an excuse as any to spend time with her. "That's the plan. I'll only be a few more hours if you're sure you don't mind waiting."

"I'm sure. Now that I know I don't have to do this alone, I can handle it."

She was more than okay. She was exceptional in every way. Tonight, he'd convince her of that.

After upsetting the dogs with her freak-out, Laylee spent some time in the backyard playing with them. They were great at chasing a ball. Maybelline always brought it back, but Tank tried to eat it. They were such awesome furry goofs.

She loved that she lived side by side with her sister. When Skye had married Ford, her next-door neighbor, she'd moved into his house, leaving her own empty.

Laylee wasn't one to let a prime opportunity pass, so she'd quickly talked Skye into selling her the house and now had access to her twin every day. Well, except for now, while Skye and Ford were on a much-deserved getaway.

Without Skye, Laylee knew she'd spend most of her time utterly lost.

As everyone had always told her, Skye was the smart, serious twin. The one you could count on. Levelheaded, capable. She was a sister and a best friend, a confidante and, at select times, a co-conspirator. In short, Skye was the absolute best.

Laylee was just described as "beautiful and fun-loving." Which basically equated to "fun-loving" because, after all, they were identical twins.

Sure, there were some subtle differences in their looks. Skye wore her hair styled differently—or more aptly, it wasn't styled. Skye just let it hang while Laylee couldn't imagine going out without first smoothing her long hair so that it perfectly framed her face. Skye was much more conservative in her clothing choices, too. Her sister was subtle and classy, while Laylee was colorful and bold.

And apparently, far too needy.

Ugh.

She really needed to get over herself.

Going to a window, she looked out at the backyard. After the recent storms, it was messy. She needed to clean up some branches. It was such a hot, humid day, though, she didn't feel like working. The mess would still be there a few days from now, when the forecast claimed they'd have milder weather.

She didn't know how Knox could bear working on a roof, but then, he amazed her daily. He was lean from physical labor, but also remarkably strong. His dark hair was a little too long, but she loved it. Almost as much as she loved his dark eyes.

He was one of the funniest guys she'd ever met and had such a remarkable group of friends. They were the kind of people you met and immediately liked. He and Ford were really tight, but they were also super close with Marcus and Bray.

They were all different. Ford was a polished pharmaceutical rep who also happened to have a big heart. Bray, as an MMA fighter, was all muscles and protectiveness. Marcus was a cop who seemed determined to save the world. All great guys, all handsome, and their wives were equally likable.

But from the start, there'd been something special about Knox.

Well, aside from the fact that he was the only single one of the group.

She trusted Knox the most. From the moment she'd met him, she'd felt . . . something. As she'd never felt it before, she couldn't quite name it. Around him she was comfortable; she didn't stress over the need to look her best or worry when she didn't understand something. He brought contentment, and she often borrowed some of his confidence.

Sighing, Laylee wondered why he hadn't made a move. Most men would have by now. She knew Knox was attracted to her, or at least, he gave every indication he was. So far though, he'd stuck to being "hands off."

Now of course, after her call, she doubted he'd ever take that big step. After all, what man wanted to take on such responsibility? She wasn't even sure she wanted to take it on.

Trying to outrun her thoughts, she opened the back door and turned to call the dogs. Since they were right behind her, she didn't get out a single word. They nearly tripped her on their way out.

Smiling, she followed them onto the porch. Tank, the little rascal, was already barking at a squirrel that heckled him from high up in a tree. Maybelline stood there watching, her gentle gaze going from the squirrel to Tank and back again.

Groaning, Laylee dropped down to sit on the porch yoga style. "Oh, Maybelline, I think I've scared him off for good. I should have just taken the damn test. But no, I had to go and confide in Knox."

Maybelline, the big lug, heard the sadness in Laylee's voice and came to sit beside her, nearly knocking her over. Tank, unwilling to be left out, raced across the yard and scrambled onto her lap.

The dogs were amazing. "You guys." She hugged them both. "You realize we're now sitting outside in this miserable heat instead of enjoying the air-conditioning inside." They didn't seem to care. She'd probably gotten a dozen bug bites already.

It was another twenty minutes before she worked up the energy to move. She got the dogs in gear by asking, "Who wants a treat?" Now that she was layered in sweat, she'd need a shower before Knox arrived, and it wouldn't kill her to repair her hair and makeup.

Unfortunately, the door seemed to be . . . stuck? Or had it locked?

Giving her curious looks, the dogs waited. Laylee tried to slide the door open again, but it didn't budge. "Hang on, guys. Let me check the front door." When she headed for the gate, the animals tried to follow her. "No, wait here. I'll just be a minute." Maybelline was no problem. She sat down, already panting in the heat. Tank tried his best to get around her the second she opened the gate. "No you don't!"

She slipped out and then had to listen to his furious yapping as she jogged to the front. Of course, as she expected, that door was locked. Now what? She reached for the phone in her back pocket, but . . . no. She shouldn't call Knox. What if he fell off the roof again?

What if he was already hurt?

Looking up at the sun, feeling the humidity like a wet blanket, she returned to the backyard and gave the dogs the bad news.

They'd just have to wait, but at least she had a hose. Maybe now was a good time to rinse off the dogs and just play a little.

CHAPTER 2

Knox heard a commotion in the backyard as soon as he stepped out of his truck. Smiling, he headed in that direction. Tank was at the gate barking his head off, and Maybelline's tail swung wildly in the air.

"Guess you guys heard me, huh?"

More joyous barking filled the air.

He noticed that both dogs were soaking wet.

"Whoa. What have you two gotten into?" Knowing Tank and his antics, Knox slipped quickly through the gate. After securing it again, he bent down to give both dogs plenty of love. Tank tilted up his little round head and closed his eyes in bliss. Maybelline leaned against Knox, soaking his jeans and pushing him off-balance. If he hadn't fallen against the fence, he'd be on the ground with them.

"Has she been torturing you with baths? Is that it?"

Maybelline answered with a huge swipe of her tongue along the side of his face.

"Girl, seriously, that was way too wet." Knox used his shoulder to wipe away the slobber, then laughed and gave her a hug.

That left his shirt covered in wet fur. Maybelline was a hundred pounds and looked like a yeti, but he loved her. Tank, a mixed breed, had some Chihuahua in him and only weighed eight pounds. They were an odd couple but closely bonded, and totally adorable.

"Go fetch something." When the dogs took off, Maybelline in a lope, Tank like a speed racer, Knox went in search of Laylee.

Only a few steps later, he saw her sprawled in a lounge chair on the back porch, as soaked as the dogs and looking pitiful. Head tipped back with her eyes closed, her wet top and shorts clinging to her curves, beautiful legs stretched out in front of her and hands laced together on her stomach, she was quite the sight. More than enough to cause his heart to skip a beat.

For a few seconds, Knox just looked at her, but when she didn't stir, he grew concerned. "Hey."

Lazily, one eye opened. "Have I died yet? Maybe melted? Please tell me you have your keys to get in."

That didn't make any sense. "Yes, I have my keys." To savor the moment, Knox approached her slowly. With her long blond hair slicked back, her perfect features were even more noticeable. High, smooth cheekbones. Arched brows. That tempting mouth that could be so sassy.

Her dark blue eyes took his measure. "Why are you looking at me like that?"

That had to be a joke. "You look hot."

"Duh. I'm roasting."

"I meant . . ." No, hold that thought. Now was definitely not the time. "You want to tell me what's going on?"

"Oh, yeah, well, I'm almost ashamed to admit it, but I locked us out."

Knox drew himself up. "When?"

"Not long after we spoke."

No way. "Laylee, that was hours ago."

"Yup, believe me, I'm aware. The pooches and I have been out here killing time. It's hotter than Hades, but the hose helped."

She gestured to the yard. "Plus, I cleaned up the mess from the storm. I mean, why not? I would have put it off, you know, but I grew tired of my own company, and the dogs wouldn't play anymore. It was either clean up the yard or cry."

Frowning, Knox squatted down by her chair. "Why didn't you just call me?"

"You were working, and you'd already fallen off the roof once." Suddenly sitting forward, she said, "Knox. You fell off the roof."

Had she only just remembered? He hid his smile. "As you can see, I'm fine. Probably fared better than you."

"Knox," she softly chided, lightly brushing her fingertips below a long scratch on his neck, then a few more on his forearms. Wearing a tortured expression, she said, "I'm so sorry."

The second he felt her touch, his body kicked into hyperdrive: breathing deeper, skin warmer, heartbeat racing. Once she'd sat forward, they were close. *Kissing* close.

The temptation to put his mouth to hers, to finally taste her, to show her how good they'd be together, was so strong he could barely resist.

Timing won out. Right now, it was all wrong. Laylee was wilted, worried, and he could tell that she was drawing unfavorable comparisons between her ability to withstand the heat and his. Yes, he'd worked under the hot sun, but that was his job, one he loved. He'd put on roofs in worse conditions, as had his father, who'd started the business.

Laylee wasn't into construction. She was a tall, slim woman with soft skin and manicured nails, not a man who labored for a living.

"It wasn't your fault that I lost my footing. I was practically raised on a roof. The fall was just one of those freak accidents."

She huffed in disbelief, making him grin.

"Seriously, my dad supported our family with his roofing company. As soon as I was old enough to hold a hammer, he was teaching me the proper way to nail down shingles. Used to make my mom nervous."

"Gee, I can't imagine why." A teasing mood was better than guilt.

"Dad never let me fall, but through the years he taught me a lot of usable skills." He'd also taught Knox, along with his siblings, the importance of commitment, the awesomeness of having a family you loved, and the value of doing your best. "The house we worked on today was small enough that the job didn't take long. The last hour was just cleanup and writing out an invoice."

"Thanks for making me feel better."

To ensure he wouldn't do anything rash, like jump the gun and kiss her, Knox stood. Catching her hands, he hauled her to her feet. "My pleasure. I'm glad you had some shade, but you have to be getting hungry. And where are your shoes?"

"I left my sandals inside."

"You could have stepped on a bee or a prickly weed, or—"

She smiled. "I didn't, Dad, so stop fretting."

Oh, hell no. "Wrong category, honey. I'm feeling far from parental here, believe me."

Her brows lifted. "Do tell."

"Maybe later. For now, the beasts want out of this heat and so do I." He kept one of her hands clasped in his and whistled for the dogs.

"I promised them treats," she whispered. "Right before I found out the door wouldn't open."

"They're understanding pooches. I'm sure they've forgiven you." Together, with the dogs dancing around them, they walked to the gate. He realized they didn't have leashes handy because Laylee hadn't planned to get stuck outside. And now that both dogs were waiting, he'd feel like a jerk if he left them in the backyard while he ran around front to unlock that door. "I need to get a key to the back door, too."

"Okay."

She'd spoken without a moment's hesitation. It *was* a good idea—in case something like this ever came up again. Did she know he didn't have the key to any other woman's home? That he'd never wanted one? Probably not, because she didn't see their relationship the same way he did. "Maybelline will follow. She's well-mannered." He paused to scoop up Tank. "But you, you little miscreant, will get a lift."

Naturally, Tank didn't mind.

Once inside, Laylee tipped her head back and said, "I'll never again take air-conditioning for granted."

Damn, she was beautiful. "I'll get the dogs their treats. Why don't you sit down?"

"As sweaty as I am? No way. Shower first." She headed for the kitchen. "And I'll get the treats because you worked."

He beat her to it, then held the treat container out of her reach. Since they'd been sharing the duty of watching the dogs, he knew his way around her kitchen. Her living room, too.

It was the bedroom that interested him most, but he hadn't yet been invited there.

Now, with her frowning at him, he said, "You also worked, not only taking care of the dogs, but your house, too, and then you cleaned your yard." He turned, saw both dogs impatiently waiting, and laughed. "Sorry, guys. Had a dispute to settle." He got out a big treat for Maybelline, and a smaller, softer one for Tank.

They grabbed their snacks and went to their favorite corner of the kitchen—together—to indulge.

"Fine. You won that one," she conceded. "But don't think you're always going to win."

He wouldn't—not until he'd won her.

Never had she known anyone like him. Once Laylee had showered and somewhat repaired her hair, she put on a touch of makeup and, wishing she could read Knox's mind, went to find him.

He was seated at the kitchen table, a bottle of cold water in front of him, absently massaging the back of his neck.

"You're hurt!"

Glancing up, he said, "No, I'm not." His gaze skipped over her, taking in her pretty sundress and still bare feet. "Feel better?"

"Yes." Drawn to him, she stepped up behind his chair and again checked the scratch on his neck. Up close, she could see it was much deeper than a normal scratch, disappearing beneath his shirt. "This looks angry." Carefully, she edged away the neckline and peered at his hard, tanned shoulder. Her wince came automatically. "You need to clean it and get some ointment on there."

His skin was hot to the touch, a little damp, and as she breathed in, she caught the scent of sunshine and man. *Heavenly.*

Another scratch at the top of his ear had her smoothing her fingers into his hair, relishing the thickness of it as she lifted it away to assess the damage. "How many scratches did you get?"

When he didn't answer, it dawned on her that he'd gone completely still. Because he liked her touch, or because it made him uncomfortable?

She stepped back, he twisted to see her, and . . . holy smokes. No, that wasn't discomfort in his eyes. Dark as they were, they practically glowed with heat.

The way he held her gaze made it difficult for her to breathe.

Slowly, he stood, and she realized his breathing had deepened, too.

She thought he might kiss her, but then he growled, "Okay if I use the shower, too?"

Words got stuck somewhere in her throat, so she only nodded.

"Thanks."

And just like that, he broke away. Both dogs became alert, watching as he went out the front door, but relaxing when he returned less than a minute later with a small overnight bag. Without another word, he disappeared into her bathroom.

Laylee stood there until she heard the shower start; then she looked down at Maybelline. "I didn't dream that, right?"

Tank barked.

"You're a guy," she said. "You wouldn't understand."

Maybelline, however, totally got it, given the affectionate way she looked at Laylee and how she tilted her head.

"He has a bag with him. That can't be a coincidence." Then again, as sweaty as he likely got when working on roofs, maybe he kept a change of clothes with him for days like today.

Apparently, Knox was a quick shower guy. No more than fifteen minutes had passed when he reentered the kitchen—shirtless.

Okay, sure, she'd seen him that way before. She'd been swimming with him in Ford's pool next door, and often when she was hanging out with Knox and his group of friends, all the guys lost their shirts.

Still, this was the first time she was alone with him, in her home, and in a kitchen that seemed to shrink in size with the two of them occupying the same space. Where did all the oxygen go?

The heat remained in his eyes as he pulled out a chair from the table and straddled it. Then he lifted a tube of ointment. "Do you mind? There are a few scratches I can't reach."

Oh. *Oh*. "I can do that," she said, but she sounded croaky. Laylee took a bracing breath and stepped behind him. It would be easier if she wasn't looking him in the eyes. *Get hold of yourself.* She was the fun twin, after all. The one who played without ever getting serious.

Guys did not rattle her, not ever.

She'd had more than her fair share of male interest, and she'd never had trouble brushing it off. She was not an overly serious person—except that she did have a pregnancy test to take.

Getting herself in gear, she removed the cap on the tube of ointment and squeezed a small amount on her finger. When she looked at his back, her heart almost stopped.

"Knox!"

Keeping his gaze averted, he asked, "What?"

"You're covered in scratches . . . and damn it, bruises, too!" His back looked painful, whether he acted hurt or not. "You should have gone home and iced . . . everything."

He actually laughed. "It's a few bruises, honey. Nothing serious."

Her eyes widened, both at the endearment and the dismissal of his injuries. "Listen up, honey," she quipped right back. "It *is* serious."

"The bruising will be gone in a day or two. Nothing is broken, and it doesn't even hurt."

"Liar," she returned. Then she oh-so-gently dabbed the ointment on the worst of his scratches, wincing the entire time.

Knox turned his head to watch her for a moment or two, smiled, and faced forward again. "When you're done, you should do that test so you can get it over with, and then we'll figure out dinner. I was thinking maybe a pizza."

Her hand shook a little. "And if I'm pregnant?"

"We still have to eat. I don't know about you, but challenges always make me hungry."

"I think a pregnancy would be a little more than a challenge for me." She finished treating his back and moved on to the marks on his neck and arms.

"I'm just saying—I'm here with you. Whatever the test says, that won't change."

What did that mean, though? That he'd remain her friend? That he'd help her figure out the difficulties? That he'd stand beside her, no matter her choice?

However he meant it, his statement struck Laylee's heart in a way she hadn't experienced before. She didn't mean to, but an overload of emotion had her leaning forward, embracing him from behind in a very gentle hug. "Thank you, Knox. You really are the very best."

CHAPTER 3

Standing in the bathroom—with Knox, thank God—Laylee looked at the test results and her jaw dropped open. "A faint line, in the wrong place." She looked up at Knox. "What does that even mean?"

"I don't know." He put one arm around her and drew her in close, then picked up the little paper pamphlet that had come with the test and concentrated on reading the details.

"A dark line with a faint line means you're pregnant," she said a little hysterically. "A single line means not pregnant. It says nothing about a barely there line on the wrong damn side of the test!"

"Shh." Absently, he kissed her temple and continued reading.

Laylee was shocked into silence. Panicked silence, but still—Knox had just kissed her. It sucked that it was a platonic, sympathetic kiss. Still, she'd felt his lips, and that was what mattered.

Then he said, "Here." He laid the paper flat and pointed with a finger. "The test failed."

"Failed? *Failed!* Why would it do that?" She'd expended so much energy just taking the blasted thing, convincing herself that no matter, it'd be fine. She'd be fine. Everything was freaking fine. "Knox, I don't have another test!"

He wrapped both arms around her and pressed her head to his chest. "We'll get another test."

"I want it over with."

"I know. We need to walk the dogs, so let's walk them a few blocks to that little pharmacy nearby."

"You said you were hungry."

Leaning back, he cupped her face and said, "I understand, Laylee. I really do." His thumbs soothingly coasted over her cheekbones. "This is big, and I know it, but I'm promising you, we'll get it figured out tonight."

"You're too blasted wonderful—you know that, right? People like you don't exist."

His slight smile made her feel better. "Look, the dogs are worried."

She turned and there they were, crowded into the bathroom doorway, both of them wary.

Tears blurred her vision, but she blinked them away and went to her knees before them. "You two, I'm fine." She embraced Maybelline, aware that the dog's fur was still slightly damp, which meant now she'd smell like wet dog, too. Then she lifted Tank and kissed the top of his little round head. At least he, with his shorter fur, was dry. "You guys want to take a walk?"

Worry shifted to excitement. Maybelline gave a giant *woof* and Tank turned three circles. Always, at the most frustrating times, the dogs could make her laugh. "A walk it is."

Knox offered her a hand, which she accepted to stand. "You're good with them," he said. "Do you remember how you used to be afraid of Maybelline? Now she's your gal pal."

"I was such a coward. She's just so big, it took a little time to get used to her, especially with the way she grumbles."

"Sounds like low growling, I know, but it's just her way of murmuring."

Everything was easier with Knox. And she was being selfish.

"You worked all day, and then you come home to me being a mess." She got the leashes, and said, "If you want, we could eat at the park first. I know you're hungry."

"I think you'd rather get the test over with, right? Waiting to eat another hour won't kill me. We'll walk, buy the test—or maybe a couple of them this time, just in case—then I'll order a pizza and it'll be here by the time we come home. You can do the test, we'll learn the results, and then either way, we'll eat."

He was assuming that no matter what, it'd all be fine and dandy. He had so much faith in her.

Ten minutes into their walk, she asked, "What if I'm pregnant and decide to have the baby?"

Without a moment's hesitation, he said, "You'll be an amazing mom. Skye will make a superior aunt, and Ford will love being an uncle." He nudged her with his shoulder. "And I'll still be here, unless you tell me to get lost."

Get real. That'd never happen. She already relied on Knox far too much. "Like another uncle, huh?" Her problem was that she wanted more, and she didn't see how a baby from another man would fit into that picture.

"No," he said, "definitely not an uncle. I'd prefer—" Before he could say anything else, Maybelline lunged to the side to happily sniff something interesting, and Knox stumbled. He laughed. "Get your nose out of that, Maybelline. It looks like a horse came through here."

"People are rude, not to pick up their dog's messes."

He shrugged. "I'll assume someone forgot their disposal bags. Or it could be some poor stray dog."

Tank investigated too, then lifted his leg and peed on it.

They both laughed and started walking again. The day was still far too hot and humid for comfort, but now a breeze stirred the air and clouds blocked the grueling sun. They passed plenty of kids playing in their yards, and then, farther up the street, a playground where some moms and dads sat on benches while their children used the swings and slides. Other parents were busy helping their toddlers with various things, and out in a field some boys were kicking around a soccer ball.

Kids. They were pretty wonderful, right? Not that she knew a lot about them—except that she once was one. She knew they were loud; she could hear them now, shouting and laughing. Messy, too; every kid she saw on the playground was sweaty, with dirty feet and probably dirtier hands. As she saw one dad use a tissue on his son's runny nose, she accepted that they got sick. Another was making demands, a few needed nonstop attention. . . .

But there was also a girl laughing from atop her dad's shoulders. Another hugging his mom and giving her a kiss on the cheek before taking off again. A toddler laughed as a mother gently pushed him on a baby swing.

Seemed to Laylee that parenting was both give and take, fun and seriousness, snotty noses but also tight hugs and happy giggles.

"Hey," Knox said, nudging her again. "You okay?"

She nodded, saying with resolution, "I'm not going to borrow trouble, not until I know for sure."

"Good plan." He picked up a ball that came his way and sent it back to some preteen boys. "Test first, decisions after." Then he surprised her by adding, "Thanks for letting me be part of this with you."

Laylee scoffed. "There's no way you can mean that."

"I'm honored," he insisted. "Seriously, Laylee, I keep telling you I'm here. Believe that it's where I want to be, okay?"

She stared at him so intently, she almost tripped over a crack in the sidewalk. "How did I live twenty-five years and not know men like you exist?"

He answered with far more seriousness than she'd expected. "You hadn't met me yet."

The simple truth of his words turned her heart to mush and brought her voice down to an emotional whisper. "I'm very glad I know you now."

He stepped closer, shifted the leash into his left hand, and laced his fingers with hers. "You're an incredible woman, Laylee. An all-around impressive person. Smart, beautiful, sexy, adaptive, accommodating, and fun."

Wow. "All that?" she teased, both flattered and a little embarrassed. The comments on her appearance she was used to. On her character, not so much.

"All that and more." He squeezed her fingers. "Never let anyone tell you different."

Speechless, she considered his words as they walked along, shoulder to shoulder, with the dogs happily trotting ahead of them at the ends of their leashes.

In this moment with Knox, the day no longer felt so hot. Her burdens were lighter, and her situation didn't seem as alarming. Not because she could unload on him, but because of the way he saw her. She was accommodating, especially with Skye. Her sister was also her best friend, and she'd do anything for her.

Yes, she sometimes leaned on Skye, but the reverse was occasionally true as well. She and Skye had grown up with their family always playfully comparing them, with her cast as the beautiful one and Skye the smart one. She didn't fault her parents; both she and her twin were well loved and cared for. But sometimes parents didn't realize how their words hurt.

The realization gave her plenty to think about for a few minutes. Of course, she also thought about Knox.

He was one of those family guys, loyal clear through to his soul, dedicated to his parents, siblings—and his friends.

And now she was one of them.

That meant something, was a testament to her and her character. Where she often felt selfish and flighty, Knox apparently saw only the best in her. That helped her to see the best in herself, too.

She was lost in thought until they reached the quaint little pharmacy. Laylee hesitated outside. In a low whisper, she said, "I'm glad I've never shopped here; otherwise they might know me."

"Want me to go in instead?"

"You'd do that?"

"I have a sis, remember? I've bought tampons and wine at the same time when she was in need."

Laughing, Laylee said, "You must be the best big brother ever."

"On occasion. Other times, I totally screw up." He shrugged as if that was to be expected. "So what do you say? Want to control the beasts while I grab the goods?"

"I say you're awesome, but no." She squared her shoulders and handed him Tank's leash. "I can do this."

"Hell yeah, you can." He stepped into the shade of the entry's overhang and squatted down to offer the dogs water from their travel water cups. "The gang and I will be right here waiting for you."

She nodded, resisted thanking him again, and made herself go through the door. Chilly air-conditioning hit her, and as she pushed her sunglasses atop her head, her eyes needed a moment to adjust.

There were several people inside. Up front were rows of makeup, then eyeglasses. Midway through the store, a woman wearing a white coat smiled from behind a counter. Laylee returned the smile but kept walking. She didn't want anyone to offer help. She found shelves displaying vitamins, medicine, nutrition . . . and finally family planning.

Drawing a breath, she searched the shelf until she found the test she wanted. As Knox suggested, she grabbed two.

Just as she started back to the front, she heard a commotion and wondered at it. Moments later something broke. There was an even bigger crash, then boisterous laughter, loud voices, and as she peeked out of the aisle, she realized with shock that the pharmacy was being robbed.

When he heard a commotion inside the store, Knox turned to quickly glance through the large display window. Could just be kids goofing off, or friends who hadn't seen each other for a long time in a surprise reunion.

Oddly, all he could see was the backs of a few men blocking the aisles. He didn't like it. When Maybelline nudged in beside him and gave a low growl, he decided to trust his instincts.

The urge to charge in was there, but he looked down at the dogs and knew he shouldn't risk them. Plus, they could get in the way. A woman, probably in her mid-thirties, was sitting in her car on her phone. Not knowing what else to do, Knox tapped on her passenger window.

She looked startled for a moment, then with a smile she lowered the window a few inches. "Yes?"

"I have a huge favor to ask. I think something is going down in the drugstore, and my girlfriend is in there." He spoke fast, making the explanation as short as possible. "Any chance I could give you a hundred bucks to hold on to my two dogs for just a few minutes while I check it out?"

She quickly turned off the car and stepped out. "My son is in there."

Knox stopped her from charging in. "How old?"

"Fifteen." Then with a frown, she added, "He's a good kid."

"I believe you, but I need to get in there." He offered her the leashes, then for good measure, handed her his driver's license and took a pic of her plates. "My friend is a cop. I'm calling him now. Don't budge, okay?"

Thankfully, she didn't seem at all worried about Maybelline's size. "I'll be right here. My son is wearing a Reds cap. Don't you dare hurt him."

"Swear I won't." As he again peered into the store, he called Marcus.

His friend answered with, "What's up, Knox?"

Knox gave him the name of the pharmacy, then said, "Laylee's in there and something's going down. A woman outside the place is holding on to the dogs for me. Can you get some cops down here ASAP?"

"On it."

Good friends never asked questions when they could act instead. He tucked the phone away and quietly went inside. The front of the store was now empty, so he had to presume the men had forced everyone to the back. He could hear taunting voices and the demand to "hurry up."

Peering around an aisle, he spotted three men keeping watch on an older couple, Laylee, and the kid. In a split second, Knox saw that Laylee was trying to put the boy behind her, while he was trying to step in front of her. They were each wide-eyed with worry but holding up. Laylee, bless her heart, clutched the pregnancy tests against her chest.

Then the biggest of the bastards reached for her. She stepped back and slapped his hand away, which had one of his friends roaring with laughter.

Knox wanted to roar too, especially when the insulted guy shoved the youth back so hard that he hit the shelves, teetered, and fell awkwardly to the floor.

The instinct to attack was just below the surface, but the last thing Knox wanted to do was escalate the situation. Laylee was too close to the men, and the man she'd rebuffed looked volatile.

Three to one—not great odds for him. Then again, he could draw some of the attention away from the others.

A third guy told the others to knock it off, and when he turned slightly, Knox saw the gun he held.

Suddenly on autopilot, Knox launched himself forward. He hit the man holding the gun before he could swing around and take aim. The man went down a hell of a lot harder than the kid had, his skull cracking against a lower shelf. Unfortunately, the gun fell from his hand and skittered across the floor.

Without waiting to see what the other two would do, Knox shot to his feet—and caught a punch to the chin that sent him reeling back.

Someone shouted, probably Laylee. Blindly, he threw more punches—and took a few in return, another that dazed him.

Thankfully, Bray had taught him a few tricks, so Knox was able to get in some strikes with his knee, dodge more blows, and then throw off the man who'd jumped on his back.

His right eye was swelling, making it harder to see, and he had severe ringing in his ears. While he fought one man, another located the gun. Knox lunged for him. Together they crashed against a shelf, sending plastic bottles and small boxes scattering.

The older man swung his cane, narrowly missing Knox but hitting the gun holder right across the nose. Blood sprayed and the man's legs buckled. Knox was trying to get the gun, but the robber wasn't letting go.

Thankfully, loud sirens intruded, signaling that the police had arrived.

Mere seconds later the doors were thrown open and cops swarmed the place.

Marcus was one of the first in. He rushed to Knox, first relieving the assailant of his weapon and then helping Knox to his feet.

"Where is she?" Knox demanded, frantically searching for Laylee. That was when he saw her, hunkered down behind one of the shelves with the youth, her arms around the kid's head as she tried to protect him.

Barely able to see, Knox started for her, but Marcus slowed him down. "Take it easy, slugger. You've got a hell of a goose egg on your head."

Laylee looked up, saw him, and with a sob she ran to him.

He caught her close, and the knowledge that she was okay stole the rest of his adrenaline. He dropped back to lean on the wall, willing his legs to hold him.

The boy, appearing dazed, said, "She wouldn't let me help. She wouldn't let me." He looked from Knox to the cops to the men now on the ground in handcuffs, then to Laylee. "She kept trying to protect me." And then, in an insulted tone, "I'm bigger than her!"

Knox understood pride when he saw it, so he nodded at the kid while he cinched his arms more tightly around her. "Thanks for staying with her," he said. Then he told the boy, "Your mom's waiting for you. She has to be frantic by now."

The reminder startled him, and he turned in a rush.

Marcus told another cop, "Stay with him," before he explained to Knox, "Bray's here. He has the dogs now."

"How?"

"I called him on the drive here."

Knox merely nodded. "Thanks." It'd probably be a while before he could get Laylee home and settled. When paramedics closed in on him, he knew he was right. The day had gone completely off the rails—and they still didn't know if Laylee was pregnant or not.

CHAPTER 4

Laylee had never been so afraid in her life. Now, hours later, she still couldn't stop shaking. The worst fear hadn't been for herself, though the thugs had definitely frightened her. She'd been mostly afraid for Knox. When she'd realized he planned to face off with all three men, she'd badly wanted to intrude, to try to help, but the boy, whom she now knew was named Wade, had wanted to do the same, and she couldn't allow it.

So she'd prioritized and urged him out of the line of fire. All the while her heart had tried to beat out of her chest.

Now, as she and Knox were finally able to go home, it was all she could do not to cry. Knox looked so beaten up.

Her voice sounded hollow when she said to Marcus, "He fell off the roof, you know."

Marcus, who was driving them home, said, "Uh, no. Didn't know that."

He'd accompanied them to the police station—after the EMTs had given up trying to get Knox to go to the hospital first. Bray, who apparently had some knowledge of first aid from being in mixed martial arts, had declared that Knox would be colorful but overall he seemed fine.

His poor face, though . . .

A black eye, a busted lip, bruises everywhere—he looked more like a fighter than Bray did.

Sitting beside her in the back seat, Knox put his arm over her shoulders and held her close. "That was earlier today," he explained to Marcus. "I got a few scratches, that's all."

"Then this," Laylee said, laying her head on his shoulder, feeling his warmth, his vitality. *He's okay*. She had to keep telling herself that over and over again.

Guilt ate at her. It was her call that had caused his earlier fall, and if she hadn't needed another test, they wouldn't have been at the pharmacy when troublemakers came in.

She'd told Knox so earlier, but then he'd asked who would have protected the kid if they hadn't been there. Yes, Wade probably would have reacted differently, so for that reason alone, she was glad she'd been there.

"We haven't eaten," Knox said.

"The gang's taking care of it."

Dropping his head back against the seat, Knox asked, "The gang?"

Marcus laughed. "Don't say it like that. You'll have Laylee thinking you don't love us."

Knox cocked open his one good eye to glare at the back of Marcus's head. "She needs food and rest, and the dogs—"

"The dogs are fine. Concerned, I'm sure, but Bray, Karen, and Lucy are with them. Lucy drove over after she got some food together." To Laylee, he explained, "Lucy loves to cook for everyone. No idea what we'll be having yet, but I'm sure it'll be good."

Laylee's smile was only partially feigned. She did appreciate Knox's friends, but right now she was having a hard time fighting tears.

They wouldn't help though, and crying would certainly bother Knox.

"That kid, Wade, was so pumped about meeting Bray," Marcus continued. "His poor mother was rattled, but Wade was getting everything autographed."

"Everything?" Knox asked.

"His shirt, his sneakers, any receipts or napkins he could find in his mom's car." Marcus laughed. "I think he was ready for Bray to sign his forehead, but Bray suggested a photo with him instead."

"He's that well known?" Laylee asked.

"Around here, yeah." Marcus sent her a grin through the rearview mirror. "And his popularity grows all the time."

The conversation with Marcus helped to distract her until they were home. It was late enough now that all the outside lights were on, though she wasn't sure of the actual time. In some ways, it was as if three days had passed, and in others, the moments blurred together like the blink of an eye.

Marcus got out first and was about to assist Knox, until he grumbled, "Don't even think it."

It reassured her that he moved just fine, giving her a helping hand and then hauling her close. He kissed her forehead. "You're okay?"

"Knox." She put her palm to his cheek, feeling the dark bristles rasp against her skin. "I'm not the one who got hit repeatedly."

"Not repeatedly," he gruffly complained. "You'll have Marcus thinking I had my ass handed to me."

So she turned to Marcus and said, "He was pretty amazing, actually. Nothing seemed to slow him down. I'm sure he gave better than he got."

Marcus laughed. "No doubt. Remember, I saw the other guys."

Knox said, "I took them by surprise and the older man helped with his cane."

The second they reached the front door, it opened, and there stood Bray holding Tank with Maybelline beside him. Both dogs were joyous to have them back home. Laylee went in first, shrugged off her purse on the entry table, and then dropped to her knees for some doggy loving. While the dogs were busy twisting, turning, licking, and occasionally yapping, Knox spoke quietly to Bray.

She hugged Maybelline first, embracing her so long, the dog seemed worried. Then she picked up Tank and kissed him on his head. Beyond the animals, she saw Bray clasp Knox's chin and turn his face this way and that, poke at his ribs a few times, and then lightly prod the area round his eye. Knox barely suffered his examination before griping. "You already did this. Leave me be."

"You're more colorful now, so I was just double-checking."

Even more worried, Laylee glanced up.

"He'll live," Bray announced again. "But I'm getting him some OTC pain meds—whether he wants them or not."

"In the medicine cabinet above the sink," Laylee said.

"Ice for his eye, too," Bray instructed Marcus, who saluted and headed to the kitchen.

Music played in the background, and she could smell something delicious cooking.

Since Knox was still grumbling, Laylee admitted, "I like that they're all pampering you."

He held Tank and stroked Maybelline. "Ford would be worse if he was here."

"Will they tell him?"

"We all agreed not to, which means he'll raise hell once he's home. That is, unless you want to call your sister? It would be fine, of course."

Laylee shook her head. "I'd rather not worry her." Again she leaned into Knox. "Besides, I've had you to talk to."

Just then Bray came out of the bathroom looking somewhat shell-shocked. "Getting you water," he muttered as he went right past them with the aspirin bottle.

"Shit," Knox said. "You left the test on the sink?"

Her eyes flared. "*Ohmigod.*" How in the world had she forgotten? She started to jump up, but Knox held on to her. "Too late now."

Suddenly all of them—Bray, Karen, Marcus, and Lucy—were standing before them.

After a brief hesitation, Bray stepped forward and said in an overly bright tone, "Here you go." He handed a bottle of water to each of them, then the pill bottle to Knox.

Lucy cleared her throat. "I made barbecue sandwiches, fries, and pasta salad. It's all ready now if you want to eat."

When Laylee glanced at Karen, the other woman grinned.

Laylee gave up. "Knox and I have *never . . .*" No, she couldn't announce that they hadn't yet been intimate. "That is, we haven't even dated." Of course, a date wasn't a requirement for sex, so she added, "We've never even kissed!"

Marcus frowned at Knox. "So you're not the father?"

Knox laughed. "You sound disappointed."

Good grief. They were all goofy. She said, reasonably, in her opinion, "I might not even be pregnant. That's why we were getting the test. I mean, a second test. Because the first one was faulty."

All eyes turned to Knox.

"He's a friend!" The kind of friend who'd gone the extra mile and then some. "He . . . he was with me for moral support. Just in case."

"But if she is pregnant," Knox insisted, "it won't be a problem."

Everyone seconded his assurance, all of them talking at once, yet Laylee got the gist of it. They didn't automatically expect her to embrace motherhood, and they weren't dismissive of her feelings, but they were supportive no matter what. Emotion gripped her throat and made her eyes burn even more.

In their own unique ways, they each made it clear that they weren't judging her.

How special was that? "You're all incredibly terrific. Thank you."

Bray helped her up, then hauled Knox up, too, much to Knox's disgruntlement.

"Let's go eat, and you can tell us all about it."

"Maybe she doesn't want to tell you about it, dumbass!" Knox glanced at the women. "No offense."

Lucy laughed.

Karen said to Laylee, "We're friends now, so just know if you *want* to talk, we're here."

Given the way they were all so attentive to her now, it seemed possible that even the men wanted to be included. Her sister had told her they were like that, all very close and involved with each other. From what Laylee had seen from the periphery of their circle, it was true.

They included her when she was around and when the gatherings were at Ford and Skye's house; after all, she lived right next door. But between modeling and traveling and just overall staying busy now that she was a homeowner, she couldn't always join in. Plus, Ford and Skye were a couple. Yes, she saw them when she watched the dogs, which was often as per their agreement, but it was usually in passing as they headed out to work or returned home.

At the end of a workday, they were all about each other. It was almost hilarious how much they were in love, and how happy they were with their dogs—as a family.

So Laylee had tried not to intrude too much. And yet, here she was now with a party in her house, following an attempted robbery and assault, and a botched pregnancy test, all after causing Knox to fall off a roof.

Yeah, she couldn't get over that last part. Actually, she couldn't get over any of it.

Marcus pulled out a chair for her. "Here you go, Laylee. Take a seat."

Bray nudged Knox out of the way, saying, "Drink your water, okay? You need to hydrate after all the chaos."

"I'll get your plate," Karen said.

Lucy objected. "I was going to get it for her."

"You should tell her about your dessert."

"Oh, good idea." Lucy sat beside her and regaled her with the recipe for her chocolate brownie pie. She said she'd wanted to make a cheesecake, but that took more time and was more complicated. Lucy was really into her different recipes.

With an indulgent smile, Knox took the seat beside her, his shoulder deliberately touching hers, his thigh pressed close—and it helped.

The problem, of course, was that she should be helping him, not the other way around. Knox was the one with multiple injuries. She wanted to pamper him, to show him how much she appreciated him.

Yet, at the same time, she *loved* that his friends were treating her as one of the gang.

While everyone ate the delicious food and then lingered over the decadent brownie pie with a fresh pot of coffee, Maybelline and Tank enjoyed the extra attention.

Once they'd finished, Laylee tried to pitch in with cleanup, but they all insisted she and Knox should sit and "recover" from their ordeal. Only she hadn't had an ordeal—because Knox had charged in like a true hero.

"You guys realize Knox was the only one hurt, right? I mean, I wanted to lend a hand, but I've never really been in a physical fight, and I figured I'd just be in the way."

"Smart," Bray said, nodding his approval.

Hmm. That wasn't something Laylee heard often. Skye was always known as the smart twin. Laylee was just the carefree, fun-loving one—at least, according to her family.

"Retreating when you can is always the best option," Bray explained.

Marcus disagreed with a snort, saying, "As if Bray ever would."

"Depends on the circumstances." He shrugged, shifting noticeable muscles in his shoulders. MMA kept him in prime physical shape. "I wouldn't put anyone else in danger, but yeah, if I saw an opening, I'd take it."

"Same," Marcus said, "though I'm always armed."

"He's a cop," Lucy reminded her.

That wasn't something Laylee would ever forget.

Bray regained the group's attention by saying to Laylee, "You should only engage if you're trained, or if you're not given a choice."

"She protected that kid," Knox bragged. "The one impressed with Bray. If it wasn't for Laylee, he'd have been in the middle of it, probably getting hurt."

"Scary," Marcus said. "I remember being that age and thinking I was invincible."

"Me too," Bray agreed.

Karen rolled her eyes. "Girls usually have better sense."

Knox laughed. "Unlike those two"—he nodded at Bray and Marcus—"at that age, I never had reason to fight, but then I led a very different life from them."

"You still know how to handle yourself."

He agreed with Bray. "When necessary."

"Your parents really are terrific," Karen said as she dried her hands after cleaning the table.

Lucy paused while loading the dishwasher to come lean against Marcus's chair. "His brother and sister are nice, too. You'll like them."

Did everyone assume she'd be meeting Knox's family? "I, um . . ."

"Come on." Knox took her hand and tugged her from her seat. "They'll have their way so we might as well go put our feet up."

"I feel silly."

Marcus paid no attention to that as he ushered them both to the couch. "Bray is making a run to the store. Do either of you need anything?"

Knox shot him a look, but Marcus kept his attention on Laylee.

"No, I'm fine, thank you." They still hadn't been able to do that pregnancy test, and no one was talking about going home. She resisted a yawn and allowed Knox to tug her down on the couch beside him.

As tired as she was, she didn't want the day to end. She liked being with Knox, and right now she needed him near.

"Okay then." Bray looked back and forth between them, jostled his keys, and said, "I'll be right back."

Knox gave her a knowing look. "You realize where he's going, right?"

She had no idea. "Where?"

"To get you another test."

"He . . . *what*?"

Putting his arm around her shoulders, Knox brought her close against him. "It's what I would do for Lucy, Karen, or Skye. He understands that you need to know, so he's getting the test. Everyone will probably clear out shortly after that."

Sitting there with her, chaos reigning around them, he leaned close—close enough that his lips touched her ear, giving her shivers—and promised, "It won't matter, you know. Whatever we find out from that test, I'll still be here with you. As long as you don't tell me to go."

Whatever *we* find out. God love him, he really was in this with her. She turned toward him so that now it was their lips almost touching. "Good," she whispered right back. "Because I'm nowhere near ready to let you go."

Chapter 5

Knox could feel her trembling, though he doubted she knew it. Hell, he felt like shaking, too. The events of the day had been too much.

Too much worry, too much violence, and too much confusion.

"I meant it, you know." Unable to stop himself, he kissed her forehead. "You handled yourself extremely well today, especially at the pharmacy."

She gave him a lopsided grin. "I was so damned scared, I wanted to pass out. I was furious that those men were scaring the elderly couple and keeping me from buying my test."

"When one of them reached for you . . ." Knox shook his head. "I wanted to kill that guy."

Resting a hand on his chest, she looked at his mouth. "I'm too bold. My family says so all the time. I'm sure Skye would have handled the whole thing differently."

"Probably, because even though you two are twins, you each have your own personality." He lowered his voice. "The thing is, I happen to like your boldness—only you haven't been. Not with me." He stroked two fingers across her brow, brushing back a tendril of hair and smiling. "So I have to wonder, is that because you're not at all interested?"

Her gaze shot up to his. "I'm interested."

"Hmm. Your sister assured me that if you were, you'd let me know." His heart thumped harder as he waited for her response.

The boldness he so admired came over her now. Her hand slid up his chest to the side of his neck and she shifted toward him. "So how about I let you know now?" And with that, she kissed him, carefully at first, maybe because of his bruised mouth, but when he groaned low and cupped the back of her head, she gave in and took his mouth the way he'd always imagined.

Not that Knox was passive. No way. Without even meaning to, he took over, pulling her onto his lap and devouring her mouth—and completely forgetting that they weren't alone.

"Wow, okay, I might be too innocent to see this."

He and Laylee both jumped at the intrusion. She landed back on the couch cushion beside him and Knox sat forward, frowning at Karen. His frustration was just enough for him to say, "Go away, honey. This is private."

Karen laughed. "Just wanted to let you know we're taking the dogs for a last walk so they'll settle down and sleep well for you tonight."

Marcus stepped in behind her with Lucy, leading Maybelline and Tank, who were already leashed. "No more than twenty minutes, so don't get too involved. Bray will be back by then, and we'll all get out of your hair."

Damn it, he'd forgotten about the dogs, too. "Great. Thanks. See ya."

Marcus couldn't hide his grin. "I know that look. We really will be gone soon enough, just put it in neutral for a little while longer."

Laylee nodded. "Neutral. Right." Like a sleepwalker, she got up and headed to the bathroom. "Thanks."

The second the door closed behind her, Knox said, "You

know I'm going to murder all of you." He stood, drew a breath, and got control of himself. "Seriously, thanks. For everything."

"We like her," Karen whispered. She opened the front door and waited for the others.

"No matter what," Lucy advised, "don't let her go."

"I won't." But he couldn't make any promises for Laylee.

Clasping his shoulder, Marcus leaned in and spoke low. "Try to remember that she's been through hell today, okay?"

"I'm not likely to forget."

Once they all stepped out, the happy dogs with them, Knox went down the hall and tapped at the bathroom door.

It immediately opened and Laylee launched herself into his arms, again kissing him as if she'd waited a lifetime. He fell back against the wall, taking her with him, then turned so he had her pinned.

She freed her mouth long enough to say, "It's sexy how you take over."

"You're sexy," he growled, and kissed her again. Honest to God, he couldn't get enough of her, especially when she pressed up against him, her fingers tunneling through his hair as she made hungry sounds.

Knowing Marcus was right, he eased up enough to nuzzle her neck, tease her ear, and then just held her close. "The others will be back soon."

"Your friends are awesome." She looked up at him. "Knox?"

He could have stood there all night holding her. "Hmm?"

"Will you stay?"

"Absolutely."

She drew a breath. "With me, I mean." With a small wince, she asked, "All night?"

Warmed by the prospect, he said, "Yeah. I'd like that."

"Regardless of the test results, I don't want to be alone tonight."

Would any man do, then? If her sister were home, would she

even be asking him? Honestly, it didn't matter. "I'll stay." If that meant sleeping with her, great. If she meant just for company, he was here for that, too.

"You have work tomorrow, right?"

"Giving a few appraisals, that's all." He'd arranged some time off to help her with the dogs while her sister and Ford were away. "Do you?"

"Just a few hours in the afternoon. It'll be a quick shoot for a local department store. I won't be gone long."

He gave her a lopsided grin. "I remember when the dogs would destroy the house whenever they were alone."

"And I was terrified of Maybelline back then." Her soft laugh made him want to kiss her again. "So ridiculous."

Moving closer, Knox tipped up her chin. "I met you on one of those days."

"At my worst," she complained. "I was so embarrassed."

"You had no reason to be."

"I was a mess."

"You looked beautifully frazzled," he countered. Just to test the water, he whispered, "It made me hot."

This laugh was a little more robust. "No way. You're making that up."

"How come everyone saw it except you?"

"Seriously? You must be incredibly easy."

More like incredibly hard, but knowing they'd be interrupted any moment, he kept that to himself. "I need to know the plan for tonight."

"What do you mean? You already said you'd stay."

"And I will. But spell it out for me, okay? Am I staying as company, sleeping on the couch, or—" They both heard the front door open.

Laylee grabbed a fistful of his shirt and kissed him hard and fast. "I want you. If you don't feel the same, tell me now."

Bray called out, "Anyone here?"

"Just a sec," Knox replied.

He opened the closest door and stepped inside with Laylee, hoping for a little privacy. "So we're clear, I've wanted you from the first day I saw you, and every day since. That said, I know today was a trial and it's not over yet. If you'd rather wait, I can wait." It might kill him, but he'd do it.

"No waiting." She opened the door and practically shoved him back out.

"What's the matter?"

"That's my bedroom and it's a catastrophe."

Unable to stop his grin, he leaned around her, peeked inside . . . Holy smokes, it was a mess.

"Knox!" She pulled the door shut, blocking his view. Under her breath, she muttered, "I planned to clean it soon."

Perfect Laylee Fairchild wasn't so perfect after all. To Knox, that made her even more appealing.

Laylee looked at each of the faces of Knox's friends. There couldn't be a nicer group of people. She accepted the test Bray offered. "I know you're all wondering, so how about I just do this now? I mean, if you don't mind waiting a minute or two to find out—"

"I'll *die* if I don't know tonight," Lucy said.

Karen leaned into Bray. "I'll admit I'm awfully curious."

Bray and Marcus nodded.

Knox turned to her. "You don't have to do this, you know."

"Only if you want," Marcus said.

"We'll all survive the suspense," Bray promised.

Funny how they could take a worry and turn it humorous. She gave Knox a hug and said, "Be right back." Less burdened with the possible outcome, she darted into the bathroom. A minute later, she stuck her head out the door and found everyone clustered together looking back at her. Definitely some funny stuff had gone down tonight, and she couldn't wait to tell Skye about it when she returned.

In the meantime, she turned to Knox, and he immediately

unglued his feet and came forward. She pulled him into the bathroom with her, shutting out everyone else.

"I can't look," she whispered.

"Want me to do it?"

She nodded and leaned back on the wall, trying to appear casual even though her heart was galloping and her palms were starting to sweat. She stared at Knox while he glanced at the stick. Then at the instruction paper. Then the stick again.

He turned back to her, cupped a hand to her cheek, and said, "You're not pregnant."

As her legs turned to noodles, the oddest mix of emotions went through her: extreme relief—but also a touch of disappointment.

Knox bent his knees to look her in the eyes. "Are you happy about this?"

She nodded. "I'm happy."

"Then I'm happy, too."

A weird sort of giddy laugh bubbled out of her. "And if I was sad?"

He put his arms around her and held her. "Then I'd offer to help remedy things."

Searching his gaze, she said, "You . . . we . . ."

"It's not a horrible idea, honey."

"Knox," she complained, laughing, almost weeping. Oh, he'd be far, far too easy to love. "Thank you."

For an answer, he kissed her—her mouth, the bridge of her nose, then her forehead.

Laylee sighed. "I suppose we shouldn't keep your friends in suspense."

"Our friends," he corrected, and opened the door. "Come on."

They were all waiting.

Knox stepped out with her, and Laylee announced, "False alarm. I am not pregnant." It warmed her heart to see that they all had the same mixed reaction she'd had.

Marcus, especially, looked disappointed. "Damn it, I was already thinking of myself as an uncle."

"Same," Bray said.

That prompted Karen to peer up at him. "Maybe we should do something about this."

For a big, badass fighter, Bray had the softest look in his eyes. "Yeah, maybe we should."

Whoa. Were they talking about becoming parents?

Lucy squealed and embraced Karen. "Are you serious? I was thinking the same thing!"

"Our babies could be close, right?"

Marcus grinned. "Guess we all caught baby fever real fast there, didn't we?"

Laylee didn't know what to think. "You both want to have babies?"

"Bray and I have been house hunting, and any house that didn't have room for a family was automatically disqualified, so I guess we were sort of thinking about it already."

"Lucy and I did the same when we bought our place. Three bedrooms and a yard big enough for kids was a must."

Glancing around, Laylee said, "I guess this house is big enough."

Everyone looked at Knox.

She rushed to add, "For when I'm ready, I mean. I'm not there yet."

Knox put his arm around her. "Now that we have that settled, can I kick you all to the curb?"

"Knox!"

Marcus pulled Laylee away from Knox and gave her a hug. "He's right. It's late and we've taken up enough of your time."

Despite the long day, Marcus smelled nice. "I'm glad you were here."

Bray got her next. "Thanks for sharing with us. It would have been hell, having to wait until tomorrow to hear the news."

She laughed and patted his chest, amazed that it was rock hard. "Thank you for picking up the test."

Karen gave her a quick hug. "Let's get together soon, okay? With Skye out of town, do you have more time to visit?"

"Or," Lucy said, also hugging her, "we could visit you, since you're dog sitting. Just let us know a good time."

"I'd love that." The offered friendship had her head swimming. "Thank you both."

"Out," Knox said, opening the door in a not so subtle hint. "Love you all, but you gotta go."

They teased him mercilessly on the way out, saying, "While you stay?" and "Why such a rush?" and "About time you settled down."

Laylee had no idea how to react to that last comment. Settle down? She'd barely kissed the man! Never mind that she'd known him for a while now, liked him a lot—okay, more than a lot—and trusted him completely. Trust was a biggie for her, especially because she'd recently been burned. Still, they were missing a few steps in the relationship department. No date, only a minimum of kissing, and no sex.

She really wanted to remedy the sex part tonight.

Actually, any minute now.

Maybelline and Tank wanted to see everyone off. It had been quite the day for them, too. Laylee scooped up Tank before the little rodent could slip out, but she let Maybelline do her thing. The big lug never ran off, and her biggest crime was her slobbery kisses. Not really an awful thing at all.

Because everyone was a lover of animals, they took turns bidding the dogs good night and then, finally, Knox closed and locked the door.

He turned to face her, his gaze watchful, his hands loose at his sides. For several seconds they were both silent until Tank began to squirm. Knox asked, "Do you think they need to go out one last time?"

Tank yapped and Maybelline headed for the back door.

"I'll take that as a yes." Gently, Knox took the dog from her. "While I take care of this, why don't you . . ." He gestured toward the hall. "Do whatever you need to do?"

"Right." Unable to think of what she had to do, but certain there was something, she pivoted away. Though she didn't look back, she heard Knox chuckle.

In the bathroom, she looked around, spotted her toothbrush, and practically jumped on it. It struck her that she was nervous when she was never nervous with men. Good experiences, bad experiences, memorable and forgettable—she'd had them all. So why was her pulse racing and her breath coming fast?

Sudden insight hit her: With other guys, she'd been in control. With Knox, things kept getting turned around and it was . . . exciting. How was she to know she'd like that so much when men usually let her have her way?

But she did. Or at least, she did with Knox.

Knowing the dogs wouldn't take long this time of night, she quickly brushed her teeth, removed the ruined remnants of her makeup, and brushed her hair. She thought about changing her clothes but then decided against it.

She wanted Knox to undress her.

And she wanted to undress him.

When Knox looked past the open bathroom door, Laylee was still standing there daydreaming. "Oh. Hi."

Smile curling, he said softly, "The dogs bedded down in the kitchen. Is that where they sleep?"

She answered just as quietly. "Usually. As long as it's not storming. Or I'm not up reading or watching TV." Or just being restless. "You turned out the lights and locked the doors?"

"Yeah." He reached out and caught her hand, bringing her forward into delicious contact with his body. "You okay?"

"Anxious." Nuzzling her nose into his neck, she breathed in the scent of his warm skin mixed with the humid outdoor air that clung to him. Everything in her tingled. Oh, man, she had it bad. "Let's get this show on the road."

She tried to urge him along, but Knox didn't budge, and when she glanced at his face, it was to see a hot glimmer in his dark eyes and a slight, sexy tilt to his mouth. The tingles sparked into a heat wave. Seriously, she couldn't wait a second more.

CHAPTER 6

Knox loved the way Laylee tried to charge through life—but he wouldn't let her rush him, not with this. Not with her.

It seemed like a good idea to take all his slow, smoldering intentions to the bedroom behind a closed door, before the dogs decided to investigate the whispers. That thought made him frown slightly.

He took the lead, now knowing which room she used, and once he was inside, he saw that she still hadn't tidied up. Clothes were stacked and strewn over several surfaces. A bra on a chair. Skinny jeans on the floor. Two—no three—pairs of sandals kicked here and there. A sheer sexy blouse half on, half off the dresser.

Lifting his brow, he started to tease her, but she beat him to it.

"I'm messier when I'm stressed." She quietly closed and locked the door. "And I was stressed about that pregnancy test."

He pulled her into his arms. "I'm glad you didn't make the bed, since we're just going to mess it up again."

She grinned. "Unlike my sister, I rarely get around to it. I pick up the rest of the house because, you know, it used to be hers and she was so freaking tidy." Putting on a mock frown, she said, "If you expect me to be the same, you'll be disappointed."

"Nothing about you disappoints me." Still whispering, he asked, "Do the dogs bother you when you have men over?"

One slender shoulder lifted. "I don't know. I've never had a guy over."

Both of his brows lifted.

Laylee stammered, "I mean . . . I've been with guys. Get real, I'm twenty-five. But not here, not in this house. And I was never around pets much before."

Knox looked around again. "Great. So I get to initiate the place."

Taking it as the joke he meant it to be, she laughed. "Sure. Some other day, when Ford and Skye are back and the dogs are with them, you're welcome to initiate the couch, too. Maybe the shower. Shoot, we can go for the kitchen table if you—"

Knox ended the teasing words with a kiss. Much more of her taunting him and he'd lose it. Actually, kissing her pushed him dangerously close to the edge, too. He'd been thinking about her for far too long. Liked her from the moment he saw her. Wanted her more each time they talked.

He held her face and devoured her mouth—and she let him, only making small, excited sounds and clinging to his biceps.

As he eased up, she slowly licked her swollen lips and gave him a smoky look of wonder. "You're good at that," she breathed. "Kissing, I mean. Completely blows me away."

So far, so good. He peeled off his shirt and tossed it aside. He'd left his shoes by the front door, but he lifted each foot to tug off his socks.

Laylee said, "Go on."

Grinning, he shook his head. "You need to catch up."

She turned. "Unzip me."

Yeah, progress. But once he touched her, he couldn't stop. He brushed her silky hair over her left shoulder and teased his mouth down the back of her neck. She shivered. Using only his pinkies, he eased the straps of her dress down. She wasn't wearing a bra. Her skin was so smooth and soft, he couldn't stop exploring with his fingertips, his lips. He held her waist, his fingers lightly contracting, and stepped up against her.

Though Laylee was slim, she had a curvy little backside on her. He slid his hands down, framing her hips, caressing her ass, and then moving back up to her breasts—all the while he continued to kiss, nip, lick, and nibble on her neck and shoulder.

"Knox," she groaned. "The zipper."

"In a sec." The top of her sundress came down with a tug, freeing her breasts. Damn, she had a nice body. He breathed deeper while he cupped her in his hands and let his thumbs brush over her nipples.

"Okay, never mind," she said, wiggling away and reaching back for the zipper. She got it down before he could reach for her again, then she skinned off the dress and stood before him in nothing more than tiny beige panties.

Without even thinking about it, he reached for the snap on his jeans. Unable to pull his gaze from her, he fumbled a second. He'd known she was perfect, but now here she was, bare in front of him, and the sight of her was hot enough to incinerate him.

Laylee stepped up. "Let me."

He dropped his hands to his sides and braced his feet apart. She proved to be a tease, opening the snap and lowering the zipper, while also dragging her nails over the denim that covered his erection. His eyelids grew heavy, but he didn't close them. Pretty sure he didn't even blink.

With her fair hair swinging to either side of her face, her beautiful breasts bare, Laylee stared down at him. Her slender fingers were on him. . . .

Yeah, he broke. As he stepped back, Knox shoved down his jeans and boxers and then kicked them away. Smiling, Laylee did this sexy little thing where she pushed her panties over her hips and gave a wiggle that sent them sliding down her long legs.

His brain emptied of words. All he could think was: mine, now, need, *forever*. Over and over again.

When he reached for her, she laughed, but when they landed crossways on her bed together, him mostly on top, his mouth feasting on hers, her humor died. She wrapped her arms around his neck, her legs around his hips, and encouraged him with those husky sounds of pleasure again.

Within ten minutes, they were both desperate. Knox said, "Damn."

"What?" she asked, but brought his mouth back to hers so he couldn't answer.

When he freed himself again, he said, "Protection." She'd already gone through a pregnancy scare; he wasn't about to put her through that again.

"Oh."

"Don't move."

"Okay." As he pushed off the bed and grabbed for his jeans to get his wallet, she said, "I'm on birth control, but yeah, one scare was enough, right? No need to take chances."

Knox wasn't thinking at all when he got out the condom and rolled it on. "I wasn't scared." He came back down over her but paused long enough to curve one hand over her cheek. "If you ever want a baby, I'm your guy."

Her eyes flared wide, but he didn't give her a chance to speak. He kissed her while he reached between their bodies, and seconds later neither of them was thinking of anything but pleasure.

Laylee barely stirred when Knox silently left the bed and headed to the bathroom. It sounded to her as if he was cleaning up.

The thought made her smile. If they were going to do this again—and they most definitely would—they'd need to make some arrangements. She wouldn't mind if he left a change of clothes at her house, along with some toiletries. The idea of making long-term arrangements with him gave her a sense of contentment.

Now that she'd lost his body heat, her skin quickly cooled, but she was too lethargic, too sated, to move. Knox Nial excelled at more than mere kissing. Never had she experienced anything like their lovemaking. Maybe it was that they were so perfectly in sync. Or maybe he was just that good, that special.

"You're smiling," he murmured as he came back in, this time leaving the door partially open.

"I'm happy," she replied as she lazily stretched. "And I feel amazing."

Kissing a path up her thigh to her stomach to her left breast, he said, "Yes, you do." His hands slid under her and then lifted her enough to readjust her in the bed. When he finished, her head was on a pillow and her feet no longer hung over the side. After freeing the lightweight quilt from beneath her, he spread it out, turned off the light, and snuggled in next to her.

It was the most natural thing in the world to get comfortable in his arms. Quietly, filled with emotion, she whispered, "It was a wild day, but I really like how it turned out."

Knox kissed her forehead. "Yeah, but this, with you, was my favorite part."

She smiled. "Thank you for staying with me."

Several seconds passed without a reply, and she started to wonder if she'd pushed him too far. She'd never been very good at moderation, especially when it came to her own wants and needs and going after whatever made her happy.

Knox made her very happy.

Finally, he said, "I wanted to stay. Anytime you want company or someone to talk to, or sex, I'm here for it, okay? Here for you. I mean that, Laylee. You don't have to explain, and I won't have automatic expectations." As he spoke, he trailed his fingers gently through her long hair. "But you should probably know, I care about you. More than I've ever cared for any woman. You're funny and sincere. I love how close you are with your sister and how great you are with the dogs."

Stunned by his words, Laylee didn't reply for a second. "I wasn't always good with them." *Great job, Laylee. Way to skirt the real issue.*

She wasn't sure how to respond to his declaration, so talking about her weaknesses seemed easier. God knew, she had plenty of them.

"Remember, I used to be a dismal failure with the pets—my fault, not theirs."

"You're quick to learn."

Wincing, she admitted, "I'm afraid I wasn't always great with my sister, either." It hurt her to admit it, but here in the dark and quiet, it was easy to make confessions to Knox. "I used to be jealous of her because she's so smart and levelheaded."

"So are you. Plus, you have to know Skye felt the same way. Somehow, she thought you were the pretty one, and she was just the smart one."

Laylee could hear the smile in his voice. "That's how our parents differentiated us. I was the pretty, carefree party girl and Skye was the smart, studious girl."

"Do twins get that a lot?"

She shrugged. "My dad is a twin. He grew up being the smart twin, like Skye, and my uncle was the athletic twin. But they're both smart and pretty athletic, if you ask me. I guess he just carried on with what he was taught."

"So you heard that nonsense from your folks and also your grandparents?"

If she didn't agree that it was nonsense, Laylee might have taken offense. "From the entire family, all of them, really."

Knox kissed her again, but this time it was different. Soft and reassuring, tender and caring. "You and Skye are both smart and you're both beautiful. In different ways, sure. Even as twins you each have your own look."

"Not that I didn't try to get Skye to be more like me." Sometimes she detested herself for that. "I used to tease her mercilessly about her boring clothing choices and the bland men she dated. That was before Ford, though. I heartily approve of him."

"I'm sure Ford appreciates your faith in him."

She grinned. "Did you know I flirted with him when I first met him?"

After a tense pause, Knox said, "No, hadn't heard that."

"I was awful. I think deep down, I wanted to prove to Skye that she wasn't so special." When Knox didn't move away from her in disgust, she admitted, "She is, though. Skye has always been the most amazing person I know. She's not just my sister, or just my twin, she's my best friend and the one person I can always rely on."

"What did Ford do when you were flirting with him?"

"He laughed at me." Remembering made Laylee smile again. "He saw right through me, and he made his preferences clear. Most guys are easy, but Ford wasn't."

"That's not true." Knox turned toward her, and even though it was too dark to see him, she knew he was frowning.

"You think Ford is easy?"

"Of course he's not, and neither am I. I don't like being lumped in with dunces. There are good men and men who are too easy, just as there are with women."

She appreciated his defense of males everywhere, mostly because she knew it was true. Her own father was a good, loyal man, as were most of the men in her family. Same with Knox, Ford, Marcus, and Bray. Paul, their friend who sometimes helped with walking the dogs, was equally awesome. "Sorry." Now she felt catty for the generalization. "Maybe I was just acting like one of those easy women, except Ford treated me differently."

"How'd he treat you?"

"Like Skye's sister." She snickered at Knox's huff. "It's true. He teased me, but he was still respectful and nice. I think he was already hooked on Skye, even if he hadn't yet realized it." She felt Knox relax beside her. "Just so you know, the way Ford blew off my interest made me like him even more—for my sister."

"You've got me wondering, Laylee. Have you dealt with some jerks?"

"Sure, but as you said, it wasn't just the guy who was a jerk. If it had been, I'd have easily gotten over it."

Knox went still again. "But you're not over it?"

She snuggled closer, her arm across his chest, one of her legs over his. "I am now." Loving how Knox smelled and the heat of his skin, she relished being so close to him. "I was at a backyard party with a date. My best friend, Marta—*ex*-best friend now—was there, too."

"Uh-oh."

"Yeah, 'uh-oh' is right. Marta went into the house for something, then a few minutes later he went into the house for something. After standing around the yard waiting for them to return, I followed because I had a feeling, you know? And there they were, hot and heavy in a hallway, all but screwing each other. It was . . . gross. Infuriating. Mostly humiliating."

"Heartbreaking?"

She drew a slow breath. "Not over him. Never over him." He hadn't been that important. Until Knox, no guy had. "What he did dented my pride, but what she did was worse. I thought we were close. I trusted her and then she went behind my back with *my* date. That was crushing. If she'd told me she was interested in him, I would have stepped aside—because I thought we were friends." Thinking about it made her heart ache all over again. In a mere whisper, she confessed, "I've never felt like a bigger dupe."

"You shouldn't. What they did reflects on them, not you."

"Maybe. But what I did . . ." The memory of it had her squeezing her eyes shut, but still she saw it all in vivid, mortifying detail. The worst was the way the other guests had reacted, with surprise, giddiness, and then soul-crippling pity. "I lost it. Instead of walking out with some dignity, I put on one hell of a show. The party was outside until I had such a fit that others heard. Pretty soon everyone was crammed in the house watching it all go down." Her throat went tight. "I made a complete fool of myself."

Knox turned suddenly, pinning her under him, holding her face in his hands and kissing her until she forgot about the scene she'd caused and the humiliation she'd felt.

All she could feel now was Knox, his arms braced around her, his chest hair tickling her breasts, his mouth hot and damp as he offered her the very best of distractions.

When he lightened the kiss a minute later, she was breathless and too warm and wondering if she should insist on round two.

"Listen up, Laylee. I happen to think you're incredible." He kissed her again. "Funny and sweet." Another kiss, this time on the sensitive spot beneath her ear. "So sexy you've been killing me by small degrees, and far too sensible to continue having any concern about what an ex-girlfriend did. If you don't trust her, no one else will either—including any guy she hooks up with. All in all, I'd say you're the winner in that scenario."

After several heavy thumps, Laylee's heart felt lighter. Her thoughts did, too. She *was* a winner. After all, she was here with Knox, and she couldn't think of a better place to be.

Knox turned again, bringing her with him so that she was half sprawled over his chest, held close with his arms locked around her. Once he got them settled, the covers over them both, he asked, "Okay?"

"Perfect," she whispered.

"Great. Then let's get some sleep. Tomorrow we have to make plans."

She lifted her head. "What plans?"

He pressed her head back to his shoulder. "Plans to spend more time together."

"Oh." Nearly overcome with exhaustion, she sighed happily. After a big yawn, she closed her eyes. "That totally works for me."

CHAPTER 7

The time passed in a blur of happiness.

Ford and Skye would be home in only one more week. Laylee had missed her sister, of course she had, but with Knox staying over each night, she hadn't dwelled on Skye's absence as often as she'd thought she would.

She and Knox went on casual dates that included the dogs, like visiting parks, having picnics, and taking long walks. Dinners were together at her house.

Each night, one of them cooked or one of them picked up carryout. It was heavenly. They'd fallen into such a comfortable routine that she wanted to embrace it and hold on tight.

This morning she'd had two photoshoots, and Knox had a few roof repairs. The dogs had been home alone, but they were better about chilling out when she had to be away for a few hours. Fortunately, it wasn't a long day.

She knew she had it bad.

When she was with Knox, she felt like she could conquer the world. When she wasn't with him, all she did was think about him. Twice today at the photoshoot, the photographer had to remind her to hold a thoughtful expression instead of smiling so much. She'd laughed with happiness, and for the first time that she could ever recall, she'd had to really work to get the look he wanted. A straight face had never been so difficult.

Knox had offered to come to the house first to help her walk the dogs to the park, but it wasn't far, and she needed the exercise. He'd meet her there with his truck and a bucket of fried chicken with sides. She was bringing treats for the dogs.

They would enjoy a picnic near a creek in a secluded section of the park. There was a picnic table situated among tall oaks, and butterflies flitted from wildflower to wildflower. They'd relax, breathe fresh air, and just enjoy each other's company.

It was the kind of low-key, intimate date she'd never had before. But then, Knox was the kind of man she'd never experienced. With Knox, everything was new and different—and better.

Afterward, they and the animals would drive together to the store. He'd wait outside with Maybelline and Tank while she made a quick grocery run.

Seamlessly, they'd fit into each other's lives. Their schedules meshed, they were extremely sexually compatible, and she . . . Well, hell. She was fast falling in love with him.

For a second or two as she headed to her car, she began breathing too fast. A panic attack? Maybe. She got behind the wheel, blasted the air-conditioning, and gave herself a second to think.

First, Knox wasn't pressuring her. Sadly, that was both good and bad. Good, because she was only just learning about real relationships. After all, she'd been the party girl twin, not the settled and responsible one. But hey, now she had a house, and that felt pretty darn settled.

The bad part was that . . . she worried she might be more invested than he was. Sure, he'd said all the right things, wonderful things, things she'd memorized . . . but they'd been naked in bed together at the time. Guys often said romantic things under those circumstances. Of course, he'd also said some super-sexy raunchy things. She'd loved it all.

Second, even if she—or they—were getting serious about each other, no one could put them on a timetable. She could slowly grow accustomed to the idea of having him in her life.

Or . . . she could lose him.

Damn, she had to stop torturing herself. When her phone buzzed, she jumped. Hand to her heart, she looked around the parking lot, grateful that no one had seen her overreaction. Quickly, she pulled her phone from her purse and saw it was Knox.

Just like that, her worries faded away. She answered with, "Hey, you."

He asked, "You okay?"

"Yeah, why?"

"You sounded breathless."

In her sexiest voice, she purred, "I was thinking of you, actually."

"Good. I was thinking of you, too." Then he turned the tables on her by telling her exactly what his oh-so-explicit thoughts had been.

Laylee slumped in her seat. "No fair. Now I have to drive home, and my hands are shaking."

Without an ounce of sympathy, he laughed. "Take your time. I'm running ten minutes behind."

"If I get to the park before you, I'll head to the picnic table and set things up." She always brought an old tablecloth. Tables beneath bird-filled trees often had some surprises on them. "I'll claim our spot, and the dogs and I will wait for you."

"I don't know. Should you be back in the woods by yourself?"

She huffed. "I'll have Maybelline with me. We know she's just a lover mutt, but others won't. And Tank will make enough noise to annoy anyone who gets too close."

"All right, but be careful."

It was sweet how he still worried after the pharmacy incident. Marcus had told them the arrested men had plenty of priors, some far worse than attempted robbery, so the cops were still holding them.

"I will be. I'm on my way home now, but I should be at the park right on time."

"See you soon, then."

Love you. She wanted to say it; the words were right there on her tongue, burning in her throat, resonating in her heart. But of course she didn't. Instead, she made a kissing sound, felt ridiculous, and ended the call.

On the drive home, she kept laughing at herself. And smiling. So much happiness couldn't be contained.

Had her sister felt this way with Ford?

Did Knox feel this way about her?

One good thing about dogs, she could pour her heart out to them without fear of judgment. The second she got home, she saw Maybelline looking out the window. For a certainty, Tank would be at her side, jumping around in excitement. As soon as she got the door open, they were both there, thrilled to see her.

And she was thrilled to see them, too, but experience had taught her that all those thrills needed to happen outside, so she rushed for the back door, they followed, and they did all their happy hugs and kissing in the yard—after both dogs had peed.

Knowing she had enough time, Laylee praised them for . . . well, basically everything, but especially for not using her house like a toilet. That was a biggie. After they'd played for a bit, come inside to eat, then gone out to pee one more time, she got everything together for their picnic. The last thing she did was change into a sleeveless romper with a blue and white floral pattern, and slip-on white canvas sneakers. She twisted up her long hair in a loose, hopefully sexy-but-casual style and finished off the look with white-framed sunglasses.

In her tote bag she carried bottles of water, portable dishes for the dogs, a few treats, and the necessary table and seat covers. Knox would bring the food, plates, and napkins. And of course himself. That was the best part.

The dogs behaved perfectly on the walk. They had almost reached the park when she ran into Paul, their friend and a professional dog walker. He was with another guy, and at first they didn't notice her because they were too focused on each other. Laylee felt like teasing, so she let out a loud wolf whistle that gained the attention of both men—and the terrier they had on a leash.

Maybelline noticed the terrier then too and immediately lowered her ears and started wagging her tail. Tank, as usual, went into a fit of barking.

"You," Paul said with a laugh, dragging along his date—and yes, she could tell he was a date.

"Um . . ." The other man held back as he eyed Maybelline.

"She's a sweetheart," Paul swore. He went to his knees to greet Maybelline. Tank was too busy yapping at the new guy.

Laylee held out her hand. "Hi. I'm Laylee, a friend of Paul's, introduced through Ford and Knox. Do you know them?"

He took her hand. "I'm Ryan, and no, I don't know many of Paul's friends yet. We only met last week."

"Ah, well then, I won't keep throwing names at you. I've known Paul longer than that, and he's been a godsend." While Paul gushed over Maybelline, she picked up Tank and got familiar with the terrier, who had a very laid-back attitude about Tank and the noise he made.

She only spent a few minutes chatting with them before she told them she had to get going. "I want to get to the park before Knox shows up."

"So you and Knox, huh?" Paul grinned at her from his position on the sidewalk where he continued to love on Maybelline.

"Yes, me and Knox—and it's been *amazing*."

He laughed. "Told you it would be, but did you listen? No, you didn't." He glanced at Ryan. "She's stubborn, but I knew right off they'd be good together. I told her, I told him. At least he paid attention, but then, he was already on board."

"What do you mean, you told him?"

"At your sister's wedding? Puh-leez. Who do you think forced him to lend you a hand with everything, even though you told him you didn't need help?"

She shrugged.

"Poor guy couldn't take his eyes off you, so I told him to quit asking and just do it."

Laylee gave him a mock frown. "An attitude like that could get a guy in trouble."

"Not Knox. Not with you." Again he looked at Ryan. "He's a roofer, so he's all muscle and sexy, too."

Ryan smiled at her. "Sounds like a catch."

"He is, and I don't want to keep him waiting." She bent down to peck Paul on the cheek, shook Ryan's hand again, and got Maybelline moving.

"Have fun!" Paul called out to her.

Laylee looked back over her shoulder. "Oh, I plan to."

Both guys laughed as they walked away with the friendly little terrier.

When she reached the park, most of the early crowd with young children had left, and it seemed to be occupied by older kids now. She glanced around the parking lot but didn't see Knox's truck. Maybelline and Tank knew exactly where they were going and led her to the trail that meandered into the woods.

Once beneath the trees, it was much cooler, and she let her thoughts wander. Knox had told her he'd been interested in her a while, but she didn't realize it had been as long ago as her sister's wedding. She'd always been aware of him, so how had she missed his attraction when Paul hadn't? She was so happy now that it annoyed her to think she could have been enjoying an intimate relationship with Knox so much sooner.

He was an excellent friend, but she much preferred his current position of her number one guy. Possibly *only* guy. Was it too soon for that?

They reached the picnic table, and Laylee inhaled a deep

breath. She needed to stop fretting and just enjoy the day. Her relationship with Knox would happen naturally . . . or it wouldn't.

Maybelline immediately flopped down in the grass and let out a loud, relaxed sigh. Tank marked his territory thoroughly—at this point, Tank owned the park and every tree in it—and then he joined her. Laylee loved the way the two dogs always cuddled together. They were the cutest, most mismatched pair ever.

After she attached their leashes to a leg of the table, Laylee got out their water dishes and filled them, brushed off the table, and spread out the tablecloth. Nearby, several clusters of black-eyed Susans grew, with bright blue chicory and delicate daisies. The water in the creek was still rushing after the last big rainfall. Birds sang, a butterfly went by. . . .

Laylee got out her phone and took some photos of the dogs, as well as the scenery. Later tonight, she'd send them to Skye.

She was just sitting down, anticipating Knox's arrival, when Maybelline jumped to her feet and went alert. She stared at the creek, tilted her head, and then began bellowing.

"What in the world?" For a second, Laylee feared that the pharmacy robbers had somehow followed her, but she didn't see another soul, and there were no noisy footsteps or rustling through the woods.

Still, the dog wouldn't calm down. Even Tank was confused. Maybelline strained against her leash.

"Hey, shh. It's okay, honey." Laylee jumped up to console the dog, still looking for a threat. Shaken, she asked, "What is it?"

Maybelline continued to pull at her leash in a way she'd never done before. Her behavior alarmed Laylee even more. "Calm down, baby. Maybelline, don't . . . !"

The leash broke and the dog charged forward. For a split second, Laylee didn't know what to do. Tank was still secure and fascinated by what Maybelline had done. Knox should arrive any minute. But if there was danger . . .

Without another thought, Laylee charged after Maybelline. The dog stopped at the edge of the creek and continued her panicked barking. With her heart stuttering against her ribs, Laylee finally saw it.

On the opposite side of the creek, a black plastic bag closed with a zip tie floated in the water, caught up in the overhanging branches of a honeysuckle bush—and something in the bag was wiggling.

"Dear God." *A living thing is in that bag.* With fear gripping her throat and her stomach in turmoil, Laylee looked around, but no one else was in sight. No one to help, no one to take charge. She was entirely alone. Indecision held her until she heard a noise that sounded like a mournful cry. It scared her to death.

She knew what she had to do.

"Maybelline," she stated firmly, "don't you dare move. Do you understand me?" She rarely gave the dogs commands. Ford and Skye handled that part of their training, along with help from Paul. All Laylee ever did was feed them, clean up after them, walk them, and sometimes play with them. As she hastily kicked off her sneakers, she said, "Sit. *Stay.*"

The dog glanced at her, sat her big butt down, and then went back to staring at the bag. She was blessedly silent now that she knew Laylee was heading in for a rescue.

"Good girl, Maybelline." Even as the words left her mouth, she was stepping into the creek. The icy water rushed against her calves, but she ignored the chill. The entirety of her focus was now on the bag.

Did snakes make noises? Frogs? She'd still rescue the creature, whatever it was, but she wasn't keen on getting near a snake. One thought led to another, and she looked at the moss-covered rocks beneath the clear water. Her heart punched harder.

What was in the water?

She realized she was gasping each breath and growled at herself for being a wuss. "Get the bag," she said aloud as she picked her way across the slick rocks. "Get the bag, rescue whatever is in it—even if it's a freaking snake—and then make sure Maybelline doesn't run away."

Glancing back, she saw that Maybelline was right where she'd left her. Tank was even behaving, sitting still beside the picnic table as he watched the drama. Reassured that the dogs were still safe, she continued her crossing. Why hadn't she realized the creek was so wide? Or so deep! The water reached her upper thighs now.

Swiping sweat away from her eyes, she stared at the bag, saying as calmly as she could manage, "It's okay now. I've almost got you."

The bag was only a few feet out of reach.

The sound of her voice caused the creature to move more and she could swear she heard panting—and then a faint meow. *A cat.*

It was still alive, although someone had surely meant for it to drown. Fury pressed her forward the last few feet. It took her shaking hands a few seconds to free the bag, and as she got it loose, she realized it was heavier than she'd expected.

The poor animal had likely floated downstream and gotten stuck in the branches of the bush. With the heat of the day, Laylee was half afraid to open the bag until she got it on dry land. If the cat fell into the water, she doubted it'd have the strength to swim.

On her hurried trip back across the creek, she slipped once, almost going under and soaking her pretty romper all the way to her boobs.

To keep the bag out of the water, she straightened her arm, holding it as high as she could while she regained her footing. She was just crawling out of the creek when Knox rounded the bend, stalled at the sight of her, and then raced forward.

"What the hell, Laylee!"

She'd never been so happy to see him.

CHAPTER 8

"Cat," she said breathlessly, struggling to get out of the creek without losing her grip on the bag. "Oh, God, Knox. I think there's a cat in here."

His mind was slow to understand. "Cat?" He took the bag from her, grabbed her hand, and hauled her out of the creek. Her top, held above her breasts by a band of elastic, gave way.

"Ack!" Laylee made a grab for it, tucking herself away. "Maybelline, such a good girl. Knox is here now."

He still couldn't take it in. That flash of Laylee's breasts only further muddled him. The problem was that Laylee was crying, shaking, and babbling all at the same time.

"She spotted it, Knox. I don't know how long the poor thing was there, but Maybelline spotted it and went a little nuts. She broke her leash. I knew the cat was still alive because it's moving so I had to get it."

Yes, the bag was moving, and it all finally clicked into place for him. He drew a bracing breath. "Shh, baby, calm down." He searched the area, trying to decide what to do. "We can't open the bag here. The cat might bolt, and I don't want that."

"It can't breathe!"

Her near hysteria was understandable. "I'll make a few holes in the plastic, and then we're going to get the cat in my truck before we open the bag. Okay?"

"Please, please check on it." She could barely catch her breath, she was so distraught. "Who would do such an evil, wretched thing? My heart is literally breaking into little pieces. I wouldn't treat an insect that way, much less an animal."

"I know. I wouldn't either." He carefully set the bag on the picnic table. Laylee was right. Getting fresh air to the animal was a priority.

Anxiously, she hung near Knox's shoulder while he poked a small hole in the bag, then another, and another.

A yellow eye appeared, peering out at them while the cat panted.

Laylee slumped against him. "Oh, honey, it's okay now. We're here. We'll have you safe in no time."

The cat was so limp, Knox changed his mind about waiting and peeled away the plastic. The cat had defecated in the bag, and barfed, and the pitiful thing smelled awful.

He lifted it, messy bag and all, into his arms anyway. "Laylee, can you get the broken leash and tie it through Maybelline's collar? We'll need to secure her while we head back to my truck."

Galvanized by his request, she moved quickly.

He spoke as calmly as he could while he carefully moved the cat. "I'm going to step to the creek to cool this baby down, let it get a drink, and clean it off a little." Laylee seemed so scattered that he asked, "Do you understand me?"

"I understand." Going to her knees, she started working the leash through the dog's collar. Seeing Laylee's trembling hands, he gave thanks that Maybelline was cooperating. The dog's attention stayed on the cat and her worried whines were heartbreaking.

"I won't be long. We'll need to get to a vet." The sooner the better if the cat was going to make it. At the edge of the creek, he slowly went to his knees, saying, "Shh, shh, sweetie. It's okay." He laid the cat on the bank in soft clover. It shakily got to its feet, spotted the water, and stumbled forward to drink thirstily.

"Good kitty. Drink up." While he spoke, Knox cupped his hands in the water and tried to rinse the worst of the filth out of the cat's matted fur, while at the same time hopefully cooling it down. He wasn't making much progress, so he peeled off his shirt, dunked it in the creek, and used it like a sponge.

The cat wasn't going anywhere. It could barely stand on its own, but to his surprise, it appeared to appreciate the attention. No way was this a feral cat, which meant someone had done this to a pet.

Animal cruelty of any kind sickened him, but this was the worst instance he'd witnessed.

Laylee knelt down beside him. Very softly, she said, "Maybelline is secure and content to watch now that the cat is safe. Tank is being incredibly well behaved."

He heard the tears in her voice but didn't comment. Instead, he said, "Honey, I can see right through your clothes." He kept his gaze on the cat as he explained. "The water . . . I guess it made the material mostly transparent. At least the white parts." He felt like an ass mentioning it, but it was definitely a problem.

She looked at herself, huffed, and said, "You've seen me before."

"Not in a park, and not when we have to walk back to my truck—where there are other people who have *not* seen you." He'd just as soon keep it that way.

"I'll worry about that later." She heaved a sigh. "The cat is responding."

Knox glanced at her, but she was watching the animal. "Yeah, it is."

"What can I do?"

He knew she wasn't talking about her transparent clothes.

"You've done it." And damn, he was proud of her. "At first, I didn't know if the cat would make it, but I honestly think it's going to be okay."

"How long do you think it was in that bag?"

Shaking his head, Knox said, "No idea, but it couldn't have been all day." With their recent heat wave, the cat wouldn't be alive now if it had been in the plastic bag much longer.

"I saw Paul on the way here. If I hadn't stopped to talk to him . . ."

"Don't do that. You got here, you saved the cat, and we're going to figure this out."

For the first time since he'd arrived, the panic left her tone. "Like we figured out my pregnancy test?"

He gave a firm nod. "Together."

In the quietest of whispers, she said, "I'm so glad you're here, Knox. I was scared to death, and then I saw you and I knew it'd be okay."

"It's not the day I had planned, but I'm with you, so I'm glad, too." He'd rather go from one chaotic adventure to another with Laylee than have a perfectly peaceful day without her.

He drew his phone from his pocket, swiped the screen to open it, and pulled up Marcus's number before handing the phone to her. "Do me a favor and give him a call. Let him know what we found. Could be whoever put the cat there is still around. Doubtful," he said when he saw her stiffen in alarm. "But we should report it anyway."

Laylee nodded and put in the call.

Knox only half listened to her conversation with Marcus. To his amazement, the cat started to groom itself. The poor thing was weak, but the wild fear had faded from its eyes.

"Such a brave kitty," he said as he gently stroked one finger over its head.

"Okay, just a sec." Laylee lowered the phone. "Marcus said he can get us an emergency appointment with the same vet he uses, but it might be expensive."

"Tell him to go for it."

After she relayed the message, she said to Knox, "He's on his way here to look around. He wants pictures of the bag, where I found the cat, and whatever other evidence we might have. Then he said 'one of the guys' will meet us at the vet's office to take Maybelline and Tank while we go in for the appointment."

She sounded awed, but the offer didn't surprise Knox at all. Louder, so Marcus would hear, he said, "Thanks, man. Appreciate it."

After she'd disconnected, Laylee handed the phone to Knox and reached out, oh-so-slowly, to touch the cat's head.

Amazingly, it pressed up to her hand, stumbled, and turned to fully greet her.

Knox warned, "It's covered with—"

Too late, but then, clearly the mess didn't matter to Laylee. As the cat tried to get closer to her, she crooned to it. Accepting it, mess and all. Holding it.

Loving it.

Of course he fell in love with her. He'd never stood a chance, but the cat had just sealed the deal.

Laylee carried the now-clean cat as they entered the house and were immediately greeted by Maybelline, Tank, Marcus, and Lucy.

"This feels like déjà vu," Knox remarked.

"Minus a few friends. Bray couldn't stay. He and Karen had a previous commitment, so once I got here, he took off but he told me to let you know it wasn't a problem at all." Lucy spotted the cat then and came forward. "Aww. A calico. She's beautiful."

Laylee gave a tired smile. It was now well past dinnertime. The fried chicken, which they'd sent with Bray when he'd picked up the dogs, would be cold and she was more of a mess than ever.

Yet she didn't mind because the outcome was so amazing. "Not a she but a he. This kitty, believe it or not, is a unicorn."

Marcus laughed. "Looks like a cat to me."

"Calicos are almost always female, or so the vet explained. It's so rare to find a male that they're considered unicorns." Yet someone had thrown him away. She rubbed her cheek against the soft, furry head. "Isn't he amazing?"

"What's amazing," Knox said, "is the patient way Maybelline and Tank are waiting."

"Oh." Laylee looked down at the dogs and smiled. She wasn't used to their being so quiet. "You sweethearts. Let's not scare him, okay?"

The dogs' ears came forward in interest and their tails cautiously wagged.

"You want to see how he feels about you?" Very slowly, she took a seat on the edge of a chair. It was comical, considering that she was still wrapped in a tablecloth, which they had used to cover her wet, transparent clothes. The romper was dry now, but she hadn't felt like unwrapping her makeshift toga.

While she got settled, Knox explained. "The cat was weak but not severely dehydrated, so we don't think he was in that bag too long."

"Poor baby," Lucy whispered.

"The vet checked him over, gave him some fluids—which really perked him up—and she gave him a bath so she could check him for any cuts or wounds."

"She didn't find any?" Marcus asked.

"Nope. He's such a sweetheart that I doubt he fought when he was put in the damned bag." Lower still, Knox said, "I'd love to get my hands on the bastard responsible."

Lucy said, "I'm sure we all feel the same about that."

Once Laylee was settled, Tank jumped up to put his paws on the edge of the chair cushion and vigorously sniffed the cat. Maybelline rested her big head next to Laylee's thigh and went completely immobile, only her eyes shifting.

Stifling a laugh, Knox took a seat on the floor near Laylee's feet and stroked Maybelline. "Good girl."

The cat wiggled free of Laylee's hold and went first to Tank.

When the feisty little dog barked, the cat gave him a disgruntled swat on the head.

Tank yelped as if mortally wounded, then dropped back to the floor, tail tucked, and ran to Maybelline's side.

Maybelline's eyes shifted again; then her ears twitched as the cat came toward her. Jiggling all over, the big dog could barely contain herself.

Marcus and Lucy sat on Maybelline's other side, and Lucy picked up Tank to console him. He loved the attention, soaking up her gentle sympathy.

To everyone's amazement, the cat rubbed himself all over Maybelline's face and didn't even seem to mind when Maybelline gave him a slobbery lick. He just jumped down to Marcus and rubbed against him, too.

Marcus said, "You sure are a friendly fellow."

Curious about his new surroundings, the cat went off to the kitchen to explore, and the dogs cautiously followed.

Laylee started to worry, but Knox reassured her. "Maybelline won't let anything happen to him."

As Marcus stood, he asked, "Have you named him yet?"

Lucy accepted her husband's hand and was tugged to her feet.

"We considered Unicorn," Laylee said. "But we settled on River instead, since I found him in a creek that's actually a branch of the river. I know it might sound like a morbid reminder, but to me he's a gift. I'm going to love him so much."

Knox bent to kiss her cheek. "Of course we are."

We. Oh, how she loved that he kept saying that. Was it his reminder to her that she wasn't alone? Or was he staking his claim to the cat? With Knox, it could be either—or maybe both.

She smiled up at him and corrected, "*We're* going to love him. And protect him. He deserves that much after what he's gone through."

With a nod, Knox went to the door. "In case River decides he needs to use the bathroom, I'm going to bring in his box and litter."

"His dishes and food too, please," Laylee said.

"I'll lend a hand." As Marcus headed to the door to join Knox, he looked back at Laylee and teased, "Cute outfit."

Laylee looked down at herself and laughed. "I'm a mess."

"Oh, please." Lucy smiled as she helped Laylee unwrap the picnic table cover. "You always look great, no matter what—even when you've been doused in a creek and you're wearing a tablecloth. Seriously, it's almost unfair, and if I didn't already like you so much, I'd dislike you just on principle."

"You're so talented in the kitchen, I could say the same about you." They both laughed. "I love how you all pull together. You're the nicest group of people I've ever known."

Lucy tipped her head. "You're part of the group. You know that, right?"

Was she? The idea made her smile. "You mean because my sister married Ford, I get to be an honorary member? Sweet. Thanks."

Snorting, Lucy said, "No. Well, maybe. We all liked you right off. But I meant since you and Knox are together now."

Without thinking it through, Laylee asked, "What if that doesn't last?"

Lucy's brows shot up. "You aren't serious about him?"

"I am!" She looked behind her when the door opened, then caught Lucy's arm and said, "I need to change. Mind coming with me?"

"Sure." Lucy trailed along, sounding and looking amused. "I never used to do the girl thing, you know? I was all about the guys, and goofy as they can be, Marcus, Knox, Ford, and Bray never invited me along when they were changing clothes."

Laylee got Lucy in the bedroom and closed the door before saying, "I bet it was fun being one of the guys."

"Definitely. Still is." Curious, Lucy looked around. "This is nice."

Seeing it through a friend's eyes, Laylee took in the décor and all the clutter. "Thanks. This is the room I moved into when I was staying with Skye—before I bought the house from her, I mean.

The colors and style are all her choices, and my sis is really good at this homemaker stuff."

"Agreed, but I see your touch everywhere, too."

"The messy clothes? Jewelry everywhere?" Laylee grinned. "Skye had already dubbed this room *Laylee's Lair*, so when I officially moved in, I saw no reason to change things. The room Skye used is a little bigger, but this room is . . . me."

Lucy sat on the side of the bed while Laylee looked through her closet. "You sure have a lot of clothes and shoes."

"I know, right? Sometimes I think it's ridiculous, but what can I say? I love fashion and color."

"I wasn't criticizing. Actually, I'm impressed. I wouldn't know what to do with all those choices. That's part of why I'm like one of the guys. Give me some jeans, T-shirts, and sweatshirts, maybe a few pairs of shorts, and I'm good to go. Working in a custom print shop means I don't ever need to dress up."

"You dressed up for Skye's wedding."

"Karen helped me out." She grinned. "I just followed her lead."

Laylee chose jeans and an oversized T-shirt. "So now I'll follow yours. Jeans and T-shirt it is."

"So . . . Knox? You aren't in it for the long haul? Because if not, you really need to tell him that."

This had to be a novel experience. A female friend warning her not to use Knox? Didn't that usually go the other way around? Except . . . Laylee knew her own rep and the impression she often gave.

She stepped out of her ruined romper, then decided to change her panties too since everything had been soaked in the creek. She'd really like a shower, but didn't want the others to have to wait for her.

After tossing her rumpled clothes in a corner, she stepped into her underwear. "Before Knox, I never wanted anything serious."

"And now?"

"Now, with Knox, I'd really like it if it never ended. You can't tell him I said that, though. Promise me. I don't want him pressured into anything."

"I won't say a word, but I'm relieved. He's a family-oriented guy. Marcus says Knox has always been looking for the real deal."

"That was all of them, right? From what I understand, Marcus had to chase you down."

Lucy's smile went crooked. "Not that I fought him that hard."

"And Bray was hung up on Karen for a while before she gave in."

"True. She was dealing with a lot and was worried about dragging anyone else into her problems."

"And I know my sister started an arrangement with Ford, but it wasn't supposed to be a romance. Just convenient. Like neighbors helping neighbors."

"All true. They really are a super-great group of guys." Lucy grinned and said, "Welcome to the club."

She knew Lucy was teasing, but it was still an awesome feeling to be accepted. "Let's hope Knox feels the same." Aware of Lucy's avid attention, she finished changing and held out her arms. "What do you think? Casual enough for the group?"

"Casual, sure, but you still look like a supermodel. I bet it drives Knox wild."

Laylee burst out laughing—until Knox tapped at the door.

"Food's on the table and the animals are cuddling if you two want to join us."

"*Food*," Laylee said dramatically. "I'm starving." She opened the door, got caught up against Knox's chest, and was treated to a warm kiss.

"How are you feeling? Better?"

"I wasn't feeling bad, but yes, it's nice to get changed. I need a shower, but I'm too hungry to wait."

Lucy followed them out. "I'm sorry, I didn't make anything new. I kept your chicken and biscuits warm, and I'd just reheated the potatoes when we saw Knox's truck pull in."

"It'll be perfect," Laylee promised her. Right now, a bowl of cold cereal would have thrilled her.

Both women came to an abrupt halt when they reached the kitchen. Maybelline was sprawled out on her massive doggy bed near the patio doors, with Tank curled up near her chin as usual. The big surprise was that River had crawled right up on top of her and was busy kneading her scruff with his claws.

"Aww," Lucy breathed.

Speaking just as quietly, Laylee said, "Maybelline seems to like it."

Marcus pulled out a chair for his wife. "You don't need to whisper. None of them are budging. I think they're settled in for a while."

Knox explained that while Marcus had taken out the dogs, he'd put the cat box in the utility room and made sure River knew where to find it. "Maybelline acted like we were torturing her by not letting River out in the yard too, and as soon they did their business, they ran back to each other—Tank included—and got into that pile."

"Huh." Laylee smiled at him. "Guess I—or rather we—have a forever cat. I wonder how he'll be when Maybelline and Tank go next door."

"My guess is that Ford and Skye need to get a cat box."

They were all amused by the inside joke. Initially, Skye had adopted Tank and Ford had adopted Maybelline, but the dogs were inseparable, so they took turns, always together, first at one house and then at the other. Each house had accommodations for the animals—beds, food, treats. Skye and Ford had even fenced their yards together to make it easier.

The couple had already been falling for each other, but caring for the two dogs had made them an inseparable family.

Lucy wondered if River could do the same for her and Knox. With the wild twists and turns of her life lately, anything seemed possible.

Chapter 9

When Knox awoke, he realized right off that something was wrong. His legs wouldn't move and one arm was cramping. He lifted his head—and damn. Maybelline was stretched out over his calves, pinning him down. When he wiggled his toes, both legs tingled uncomfortably. Tank was tucked somehow between Maybelline and Laylee. With Laylee using his right arm for her pillow, he was effectively immobilized.

River . . . ? *Ouch*. Feeling claws sink into his shoulder, he turned his head and there was the cat, stretching—claws out—now that Knox had disturbed his sleep. The cat's yellow eyes opened, he gave a rumbling purr, and butted Knox's chin.

"Mmm," Laylee said, indulging her own stretch until she became aware of the cramped conditions. "What . . . ? Oh." She peeked up at Knox. "Good morning."

Yeah, this. He wouldn't mind starting every single morning for the rest of his life in exactly this way, as long as he was waking with Laylee beside him. "Good morning."

"We have company."

How could she look so beautiful and sexy even now? Neither one of them had gotten nearly enough sleep. Worse, the animals had afforded them no time for intimacy.

The cat wanted to be with them, and where River went, Maybelline and Tank followed.

At first Knox had been determined to set a proper routine. He loved animals, he really did, but he'd wanted Laylee. For that, he needed a smidge of privacy. A few hours. Hell, he could have worked with thirty minutes.

He didn't get five seconds.

Repeatedly, he'd taken the animals back to the kitchen. But they hadn't stayed there. So he'd tried moving the pet beds to the hall just outside the closed door. River was relentless, which also had Maybelline and Tank whining.

At one in the morning, he'd dragged the beds to the floor inside the room with the hope that the animals just wanted to be near them. After all, River had been through an ordeal.

But no. The cat wanted to be *on* them, and that meant Maybelline and Knox did, too.

"You're all cock blockers," he grumbled now to the sleepy animals. His need for Laylee hadn't abated. Pretty sure it never would.

"River was the instigator," Laylee said around a yawn. Carefully, she extricated herself from the tangle of furry bodies. Her long hair was messy, her blue eyes heavy with sleepiness. The oversized shirt she wore barely covered her panties and left her long bare legs on display.

No woman should look that hot first thing in the morning, and yet she did.

At the bedroom door, she asked, "Who wants to go out?"

Her question caused a mad rush of flying paws and scrambling bodies as first Maybelline—huge lummox that she was—rolled and kicked until she'd freed herself, and then Knox lifted Tank off the bed. The dogs went flying up the hall.

Eyes wide and ears back, River sat up to watch, confused by the pandemonium until he apparently decided he didn't care. He cuddled into Knox's neck and turned up the volume of his purrs.

Knox had to laugh. "Nuisance," he said to the cat, then gave him a stroke that had claws gripping him again. "Ouch. Stop that."

River rolled to his back and scooted closer.

"You're a real snuggler, huh? I wonder if a cat buddy would appease you at night."

Laylee strode back in saying, "Don't even think it. The bed's not big enough."

He sat up. "Come here and give me a kiss."

She dropped the shorts she'd just picked up and crawled into the bed to straddle his lap. After petting River, she leaned down, and Knox captured her mouth for a kiss that would hopefully hold him until later.

A useless effort, because he wanted Laylee all the time—and he didn't think that would change anytime soon.

When he pulled away, she collapsed to his side and cuddled against him much as River had. "I wanted you last night. Unfair that the animals wouldn't let it happen."

"We'll figure it out."

"I put on coffee."

He trailed his fingertips up and down her arm. "Thanks."

Smiling at him, she asked, "What do you have going on today?"

"Nothing. I was hoping to take you to meet my parents."

She sat up in a rush. "Really?"

River looked at them both, then left the bed, probably to find the dogs.

"Come on. My legs feel like lead after Maybelline slept on them. Let's get that coffee."

"I'll need you to hold River first so I can let in the dogs."

Already they were working together as a couple. Once the animals were all inside and eating their breakfast, Knox went into the bathroom to shower, shave, and clean his teeth.

When he came out, Laylee was half asleep on the sofa, her

messy hair trailing over her shoulders in long pale blond ropes. He had to grin at the sight of her. Tank was tucked in close beside her hip on a cushion. Maybelline was on her other side with her head over Laylee's outstretched legs. River sat on Maybelline's head with his paws around her neck while he purred and rubbed his face against her.

Sweet images like this were enough to make any man think about the future. He'd been doing that for a while, actually. Unlike his buddies, he'd come from a terrific background with a wonderful family. He'd seen his mom and dad in good times and bad, working as a team; he'd witnessed the caring, the support, and the love.

He wanted that, but only with the right woman.

As he surveyed Laylee's relaxed posture and limp limbs, he knew it wouldn't be easy to reach her while she was buried under pets, so he quietly asked, "Who wants a treat?"

That got a stampede going, startling her fully awake. The animals all hurried back to the kitchen, and once they had their individual goodies, he returned to Laylee and kissed her forehead. "We leave for my parents' house in thirty minutes."

She shot up so quickly, her forehead smacked his chin. "What?" Rubbing her head, she said, "I won't be ready! I assumed you meant later."

"Paul's coming over. He's interested in meeting River and said he'll dog sit for us. My folks would love to meet all the animals, but I wanted it to be a little calmer today." He wanted her to get to know his family and vice versa. It was a big first for him and that made today important. "Later, maybe in a few weeks, we'll have a cookout or something in the yard and invite everyone."

Laylee blinked at him.

Yeah, he'd just insinuated, rather strongly, that they'd still be together weeks from now. Not only that, but he'd commandeered her house for a gathering with the presumption he could invite anyone he wanted. It was a deliberate move, and he waited to see how she'd react.

She gave him an enormous smile but spoke softly. "I love that idea, and I'm thrilled to meet your family in a calm setting."

With a quick kiss, she started to dash down the hall until he caught her hand. "Fair warning. The word *calm* doesn't really apply to my family when we're all together."

Lifting an eyebrow, she asked, "So not just your mother and father?"

He shook his head. "My sis and brother, too. You'll like them," he predicted. Since he loved them, he couldn't imagine anyone not doing the same. "I just wanted to prepare you."

Laylee put her palm to his jaw. "Don't worry. I come from a big extended family, remember? You met some of them when Skye and Ford got married. But now I have to rush, because there's no way I'm going to meet them unless I look my best."

Her best was pretty awe-inspiring. Knox felt certain she was going to bowl his family over.

Laylee had the time of her life. Knox's family was very different from her own. Both were great—she loved her folks and knew they loved her, too. But never before had anyone focused so much attention on her. Well, not family anyway.

Guys, sure. Photographers, all the time.

But a mom and dad? A brother and sister? That was new and fun. She liked it, especially because she was so accepted.

Knox had proudly introduced her to Nolan and Jenny. His father wasn't quite as tall as Knox, but he had the same lean, muscular build and the same dark tan and nearly black hair, with a little silver in it. Nolan wore his hair shorter than Knox did, but his smile was equally engaging.

He'd welcomed Laylee to the family with an enthusiastic hug, as if this were more than a mere introduction, more than a friendly family brunch.

His mother, Jenny, was a pretty woman with curly brown hair, beautiful green eyes, and a smile that could put anyone at ease.

She'd hugged Laylee too, whispering, "It is so nice to finally meet you."

Finally? So Knox had mentioned her to them? Nice.

His sister, Ashlee, shot Knox a grin before offering him a high five. "Not bad, big brother. You're doing all right for yourself."

Knox laughed, caught his sister's hand, and pulled her in close—only to muss her hair, which had her swatting at him.

Jacob, his twenty-one-year-old brother, leaned in to say, "If Knox doesn't work out, I'm available."

"Not in this lifetime." Knox shoved him back, and when they started to roughhouse, Jenny smacked at them both.

"Behave yourselves. You'll have Laylee thinking we don't have any manners."

"Actually," Laylee said, "I already think you're all wonderful."

"Oh?" Jenny asked. "Has Knox told you about us?"

"Yes, but he didn't need to. Knox is pretty incredible, and I figure that could only happen if he had great parents."

Smug, Knox put his arm around her and led the way to an informal dining room. "Told you she was smart."

That was confirmation he had spoken about her to his parents, and now Laylee wished she knew every single thing he'd said.

"If he told you about the pharmacy robbery, well, I know I overreacted. And that whole fiasco with the cat in the creek . . . I admit I fell apart a little, but I was so scared for the cat, and—"

They all grinned at her.

Ashlee said, "We think you're wonderful, too."

That was how the day started and continued.

Nolan, she found, was a real stand-up guy. Plainspoken and funny, especially when he told stories about his kids. He had Laylee laughing out loud several times. He was also no-nonsense and courteous in an old-school way, especially toward his wife.

When Knox's mom went to the kitchen to get the food, his dad jumped up to help—and then so did Knox's brother and sister and Knox himself.

It was amusing, especially since Jenny took their solicitude in stride.

After a few instructions, she left the chore to her husband and kids and sat down beside Laylee to "get better acquainted."

"Knox told us you were a model, but I still didn't expect you to be so perfect."

"Oh, no, I'm not," Laylee protested. "You should have seen me this morning when Knox and I first woke up—" Too late, she realized what she was saying and who she was saying it to. Her mouth snapped shut as her face got hot. "I mean, I, um . . ."

Jenny laughed. "Moms are very worldly when it comes to their children, believe me." She added in a whisper, "Plus, I know their dad."

Laylee snickered. "Sometimes my mouth gets ahead of my common sense. Honestly, though, usually my dates don't bring me home to meet their families."

"You're more than just a date though, right?"

She bit her lip. "Maybe? We haven't really discussed the future."

Jenny didn't put her on the spot—at least not more than she already had. "Now you know what you're in for. We're a close family and I don't want that to change, so if I ever make you uneasy, please just let me know."

"You couldn't," Laylee promised. Then thought to add, "Thank you."

As Nolan came in carrying a big dish, he said, "You're in for a treat, Laylee. Jenny made her famous ham and cheese casserole."

"It smells delicious."

"If you like it," Ashlee said, "have Knox make it for you. Mom made sure we could all cook." She set a fruit platter on the table.

"Knox is better at it than I am," Jacob claimed, as if selling the merits of his brother. He carried two different pitchers of juice. "I can get by, and Ashlee does okay—"

Ashlee deliberately bumped him, almost making him spill the drinks.

"—but Knox could be a chef."

"Thanks," Knox said, "but you're still doing the dishes."

Laylee could have been overwhelmed, especially with all of them joking and including her as one of their own, but instead she just enjoyed herself.

Toward the end of the meal, Nolan and Knox were discussing a roofing job, and Ashlee chimed in.

"Do you do roofing, too?" Laylee asked.

"I've pitched in, but I don't love it the way Knox does. If I had your looks, I'd be a model. That sure seems easier."

Nolan immediately protested. "You should know better," he scolded. "No job, when done well, is easy."

"I don't know," Laylee said. "It does seem easier than laboring in the hot sun, but you're right, modeling does have its challenges. Long hours, forced smiles, *really* uncomfortable shoes, travel when it's not convenient, constant criticism . . . Once, when I hadn't slept well, the photographer kept complaining and asking for more and more and more makeup because I was washed out. All I wanted to do was go home and sleep."

"I didn't know that," Knox said.

She shrugged. "We've never really discussed my work." The idea of her modeling seemed silly sometimes. Most of the men she'd dated had made it out to be a big deal, carrying on as if they'd scored something special. But not Knox.

He definitely made her feel special, but not because of her looks, or because she modeled.

With him, she was just herself.

Knox frowned, as if lost in thought.

Nolan broke the sudden silence by saying, "I raised my daughter much like my sons. I wanted her to be self-sufficient so that she'd never 'need' a man. I'll be happy when she finds a keeper, but it will be because she loves him, not for any other reason."

"He tells me that all the time," Ashlee said. "Mom just tells me to be happy."

"I want you all happy," Nolan protested.

"Happily independent," Jacob countered.

"Stop," Jenny said. "You'll have her thinking we only wanted to be rid of you."

Jacob leaned over to hug his mom. "Nah. Mom cried when I went off to college, but then Dad almost did, too."

"Tears of happiness," Nolan insisted. "I didn't think you'd ever make a decision."

From there, the mood lightened again, and they all talked for another hour. Honestly, Laylee could have stayed and visited all day, but she knew they needed to get home to the animals. Paul, awesome as he was, probably had his hands full and was ready for a break.

She'd couldn't have been more wrong.

"A harness for a cat."

Knox gave Laylee a hug. "Hey, I never considered it, either."

Paul grinned at both of them, his gaze going back and forth. "I knew I was right about you two."

Knox gave him a light shove, then laughed. "How much do I owe you?"

"Consider it a gift. I enjoyed getting to know River, and I always enjoy visiting the dogs."

"But you're a professional," Laylee protested. "It's your job, so we have to pay you."

"True, but I was here as a friend, not an employee."

Laylee crossed her arms. "Fine, but I'm keeping the harness."

Paul grinned. "It's a gift, too. I knew once I put it on River, I couldn't take it back."

"But—"

He put a finger to her lips, silencing her. "This is where you say, 'Thank you, Paul. Friends like you are a blessing.' "

Dutifully, she said, "Thank you, Paul. A friend like you is the very, very best blessing a girl could ever have."

"I know."

Laughing, they all turned their attention to the animals. Maybelline and Tank were running around the yard, constantly finding things to bring to River—a twig, a dandelion, or one of their many toys. From a lawn chair, River regally watched over them. He wore his harness as if it had always been on him. The attached leash was secured to the arm of the chair. If the cat decided to escape, he wouldn't get far, but this way he could enjoy the yard with the dogs.

"I'll need to set up a lead for him," Knox said. "Maybe something hooked to that biggest tree so he can lounge in the grass when he wants."

"We took a test walk," Paul explained. "Just around the perimeter of the combined backyards. It was hilarious. Maybelline kept checking that River was still there, and Tank ran circles around us. The dogs loved it, but we'd only finished half of the walk when River decided he'd rather be carried."

"He looks happy," Laylee said softly.

"So do you." Paul drew her in for a tight hug. "You've quickly become one of my favorite people, now more than ever." He put a loud smooch on her forehead. "Thank you for being awesome."

Knox saw the expressions shifting over her face, pleasure and modesty, a touch of embarrassment over the praise.

"Thanks, but I'm not—"

Before she could reject the compliment, Knox said, "Yes, you are. And then some."

It struck him that she truly didn't realize how others valued her. This drop-dead gorgeous woman who would do anything for her sister would also risk herself during a robbery to protect a youth she didn't know. She was polished and manicured but hadn't hesitated to wade into a muddy creek to rescue a stray cat. She mingled easily with his friends and family, while also being a high-demand local model who easily supported herself and an independent lifestyle.

She had all that going for her and yet she compared herself to her twin sister and somehow found herself lacking. Remarkable.

Of course he'd fallen in love with her. How could he not?

This time, Paul shoved Knox, interrupting his deep thoughts. "She's a catch, and don't you forget it or you'll answer to me."

"Yeah, she is."

"You're the whole package too, Knox. Rugged, handsome, and smart." He winked at Laylee. "Treat him right."

She nodded and said far too seriously, "I'll try," which had both men laughing.

After that ridiculous exchange, Paul announced that it was time for him to go.

Once he'd disappeared around the gate, Laylee said to Knox, "He endorsed us both."

"Paul likes to play fair." He put his arm around her and after another fifteen minutes, they brought the animals inside and fed them. Knox considered putting the pets outside again while he showed Laylee, once more, just how perfect they were together, but he knew she'd worry. And honestly, so would he.

The backyards were securely fenced, but Tank could be tricky, and it was still hot enough that neither of them wanted to leave the animals outside unattended for more than a few minutes.

And he didn't plan to be quick.

Instead, they went for another long walk to visit the park, where everyone was fascinated by the cat walking along with two dogs. The pets got a lot of attention and, hopefully, enough exercise to make them sleep soundly that night.

After dinner, he and Laylee played with the animals in the yard. River chased lightning bugs and the dogs chased River. By the time they called it a night, all three were ready to sleep.

In Knox's view, it had been a long, productive day with plenty of insights and more than enough reason for him to cement his relationship with Laylee. Did she feel the same?

He'd ask her—after he spent a few hours showing her how much he loved her.

It wasn't until after they'd taken turns showering and the animals were conked out in a pile together on the couch that the humans were finally able to sneak down the hallway. Knox left the TV on to help hide any noise they might make.

Giggling, Laylee said, “You know this isn’t going to work.”

“Shh. It will if you’ll be quiet.”

“We’re going to have sex, right?”

He silently closed the bedroom door behind them, turned to her, and said, “Most definitely.”

She was already stripping off her clothes. “Then we’ll both need to be quiet.”

Knox peeled off his shirt. “I’m *up* for the challenge.” When she started to laugh, he tumbled her to the bed and covered her mouth with a searing kiss. In seconds, they’d both forgotten about being quiet, but thankfully, the pets slept on undisturbed.

Chapter 10

"Leaving on the TV was a genius move." Her heart was still pounding, her breathing too hard, and her entire body tingling. Every time with Knox seemed better and more precious.

She never wanted to let him go.

After another minute or two, he said, "Can I talk to you about something?"

Talk? She could barely keep her eyes open. But this was Knox, and she knew she loved him, so she managed a nod and whispered, "Sure."

He lifted his head and stared down at her, those dark eyes of his looking into her soul. "Your career is important to you?"

Unsure how to answer, Laylee shrugged. "It's what I do, and it's how I support myself. I'm proud of the fact that I've been successful on my own for so long."

"But?" he prompted.

Her eyes lowered as her fingertips drifted over his shoulder. "It's not really an accomplishment." It wasn't easy to talk about herself, despite the compliments she'd always gotten. "I was born with this face and body, and other than watching what I eat and getting plenty of exercise, I haven't really done anything to contribute to my success."

"Bull." He turned to his back, bringing her with him, so that now she was on top. "You're beautiful with or without makeup, regardless of what you wear or don't wear. But you have a flair that others don't. The way you wear your clothes, how you do your makeup—it's all professional and that's a learned skill. Plus, it's just now occurring to me how much exercise you get. All those long walks with the dogs, that's part of it, isn't it?"

"I suppose." She leaned down to kiss him. She couldn't be naked with Knox, even after phenomenal pleasure, and not want him again. "It's like your work on roofs, carrying loads of shingles and swinging hammers." She ran a hand over his hard shoulder. "Doing the work you enjoy has left you shredded. I enjoy what I do most of the time, so it doesn't feel like I'm putting myself out."

His brows drew together. "I hate that I didn't realize what the work involved until my sister made her assumption that it was easy."

She smiled to let him know it was okay. "Ashlee isn't the only one to think that. Most of my family think I'm just partying all the time. They consider modeling a lark." In a mock stern voice, she said, " 'You're just not serious and levelheaded like Skye.' "

His frown deepened. "Your family shouldn't say those things to you. Don't they know you at all?"

"No one knows me as well as Skye does."

Knox turned again, pinning her under him. "I want to. I want to know everything about you."

"Most of it is boring."

"Not true. Every single thing about you interests me."

Maybe now would be a good time to press—just a little bit—for more. "Ford and Skye will be back soon."

"And?"

He wasn't making this easy. "How will we explain . . . us?"

His kiss made it clear no explanation was necessary. "Neither of them will be confused."

"So . . . we'll still be doing this?"

The corner of his mouth curled. "This?" he asked, pressing his pelvis against her. "Yeah, I hope so."

She hoped so, as well. "I meant this, as in you spending the night at my house."

"I suppose that's up to you."

Now she was frowning. Why didn't he just state what he wanted? Well, she wouldn't hesitate. "I want you to stay."

"Good."

Seriously, she wanted to smack him. "Gee, Knox, does that mean you want to stay, too?" Her voice rose, but damn it, she couldn't help it. She pushed him off her and went up on her knees, ignoring the fact that she was naked. "You know, this feels like a very one-sided conversation."

He had the gall to grin at her. "I want to stay."

For how long? No, she wouldn't be that pushy. Trying a roundabout way of questioning him, she said, "You know Ford and Skye got together because of the dogs."

He snorted.

"They did! They wanted to care for them and protect them." She saw the skepticism in his eyes, but it didn't deter her. "Now we have River."

"Yeah, we have River." Knox stared at her hard. "Understand something, Laylee. I wouldn't tie myself to a woman for a cat."

She deflated. "No, of course not."

Knox reached out for her, but she tried to dodge him. Didn't do her much good. In no time at all, he playfully wrestled her down on the bed and moved over her once more. "Such a small voice for such an energetic woman."

Oh, hell no. "My voice is *never* small."

He didn't debate with her. "I can give the cat everything he needs."

"So can I."

"In return, the cat will give affection, loyalty, a few problems, of course, but I'll enjoy having him."

She couldn't think of River without smiling. "He's a sweet little unicorn."

Knox touched her chin, lifting her face. "I would only tie myself to someone out of love."

Done discussing it, Laylee nodded. "I understand."

"Do you?"

"Sure. You're a catch. Whoever wins you over will need to be special."

"You're about as special as a person can get."

Her gaze shot to his. "Damn it, Knox, what does that mean?"

"No way can you be that obtuse, honey."

She started to shove him away, then changed her mind and locked her arms around his neck. "No, I'm not obtuse."

"Insecure? Inattentive?"

Her scowl darkened.

"Fine," he said, with a lot of silly drama. "You tell me what it is."

"What *what* is?"

His expression softened, along with his tone. "The reason you haven't yet realized I love you."

Honest to God, her breath left her and she wheezed, "You love me?"

"I thought it was obvious."

This time she gave in and smacked him. "No, it wasn't, and I can't believe you didn't tell me sooner."

"Laylee?" he said with a smile. "I love you."

A high-pitched bark, followed by a deeper bark, signaled that the beasts had awakened and their private time had ended.

Knox held her still when she would have gotten up. "They'll keep another minute."

Deciding he was right, she settled against him and said, "I love you, too." It felt so amazing to say it out loud, she grinned. "I think I've been falling in love with you for a while and this past week, it just landed on me with so much clarity."

He nodded. "It was a lot. I wanted to be there for you. I hope I made it a little easier."

"Knox." She indulged in another kiss. "I'm not the only one who went through stuff. You were right there too, being impressive and take-charge and . . ." The words stuck in her throat, so she took a second to compose herself. "You were everything. More than I knew a man could be."

"And good in the sack."

The laugh took her by surprise. "Yes, very."

His slow, easy smile was so sexy. "What a relief, because my mom already told me she's keeping you."

Such a nice sentiment. "I have so much to tell Skye when she gets back home."

The barking was now right outside the bedroom door. "One more thing."

"Better hurry," she said. "They're starting to sound impatient."

"You probably realized after meeting my family that I want the whole deal. Real commitment. Forever. In sickness and in health."

Her eyes widened. "You want to get married?"

"Only to you, and only when you're ready."

"So if your family hadn't liked me . . . ?"

"I wanted you to like them, not the other way around. I already knew they'd love you."

"I do like them. A lot." It didn't seem possible for one body to hold so much happiness. "What if I'm ready to get married right now?"

"I think we'd need to wait for Ford and Skye, but otherwise, whatever you want is fine by me."

"I want kids," she warned. "I didn't. I mean, I hadn't thought much about kids until my pregnancy scare. It panicked me, but it also . . . I don't know. It made me think about holding a baby, caring for him or her, and I think the idea started brewing and hasn't completely stopped."

Without a speck of concern, Knox smiled. "I look forward to being a dad, and I'm sure you'll be an amazing mom."

She didn't doubt Knox's ability to do anything, but she wasn't so sure of her own maternal skills. "What if I mess up?"

"I'll tell you what my mom and dad taught me. No parent is perfect. Mistakes will happen, guaranteed, but love is the most important thing. Through the years we've had disagreements, but never, not once, have I doubted their love." He ran his fingers through the length of her hair. "You're already an amazing sister. Family is important to you, and it's important to me. When we take that step, I'm confident we'll do all right."

"Having a baby might make modeling a problem."

"And that worries you?"

"No, it's just that I wouldn't be employed. Not until I figured out something else to do."

"I don't love you because you're a model. I love you because you're you. I'll love you if you retire from modeling, and when you're sick, and as we both get older." He touched her cheek. "I'll love you always."

After that touching declaration, melting was a real possibility. "I like my house, Knox. I like living by my sister."

"Babe, I love *you*. The rest doesn't matter to me, so I think you're just arguing with yourself."

It felt like her heart might burst from her chest. Beyond excited, she squeezed him tight, kissed him once more, and then pressed him back. "Come on. Let's tell the animals."

Tomorrow, they'd tell everyone else.

EPILOGUE

To Skye's surprise, Laylee decided to follow her lead with a simple family wedding in the combined backyards. She even opted to wear the same wedding dress, which her sister happily loaned to her.

And because that was so easy, their friends were able to wear the same dresses, too. It was like a matching twin wedding—with a time gap in the middle.

Laylee explained her decision easily enough. She'd planned Skye's wedding for her, so naturally she loved all the choices.

Knox's mother had enjoyed helping her add some extra touches, like fresh flowers and the perfect casual menu.

Marcus attended with Lucy, and Bray with Karen. Laylee and Skye's family cheerfully returned, and this time Knox's family joined the large group. Paul, who attended with a different but equally nice date, bragged repeatedly that he'd always known they would make an ideal couple.

Everyone was happy, though Knox's mother, Jenny, cried a lot—something her kids teased her about. His dad, Nolan, merely held Jenny close and smiled.

"His family sure is different from ours," Skye said. "Jenny met me and knew right away that I wasn't you."

"You weren't wearing white."

"Ha! Mom mixed me up, then accused me of fooling her. Dad said it's because I'm so happy now, I look more like you."

Laylee grinned. "You do glow a little more these days."

"Not once has Ashlee or Jacob gotten confused, either. They've hugged me a lot, though," Skye confessed. "They said they've known Ford for a long time, and since we're sisters, they want us included in all their family holidays now."

Laylee smiled. "Knox's family is way more hands-on than ours." She and Skye knew they were well loved, but their parents were fine letting them do their own thing, assuming they'd take care of themselves and only involve them when necessary. "I'm so glad Knox had such a beautiful upbringing."

They both knew Marcus and Bray hadn't been so lucky—at least not until later, when they'd been adopted. And Ford had gone through his own childhood nightmares, which explained his early independence and estrangement from his parents.

Skye leaned against Laylee, saying softly, "I'm so glad we've always had each other."

"You're the best part of me," Laylee said, then squeaked when Skye pinched her.

"Don't say that. You're perfect and I love you."

From behind them, Knox said, "I agree." He tugged Laylee into his arms, pressed a kiss to her forehead, and said, "Best of all, you're perfect for me."

Ford, leading River along on his leash, pulled Skye to him. "This arrangement, living next door to each other, is pretty sweet, too."

"Built-in pet sitters?" Knox asked.

"For both of us."

Yes, Laylee agreed. Her life had always been pretty great, but now it was absolutely perfect—in every single way.

The Rancher's Unexpected Family

MAISEY YATES

CHAPTER 1

Ellie Parks had been living in fear of the midnight phone call since high school. Ever since Melanie had first started running around with Ty Porter and had begun her walk off the good girl path and into destruction.

She'd been waiting to hear the worst.

And while this wasn't the worst, it was shocking in a way that left her cold.

She grabbed her purse off her nightstand, along with her phone, which was never in do-not-disturb mode, all because of her sister. Then she walked downstairs, and toward the front door. And heard the sound of her roommate's door opening. To be accurate, Ellie was Angelica's roommate, rather than the other way around. It was Angelica's house, and Ellie helped pay the mortgage by renting a room. It wasn't impossible to buy a house on a teacher's salary, but it was difficult. And while Ellie was saving up for a down payment, her colleague had been generous enough to let her stay.

It was a little bit weird living with her former teacher. But then, Angelica was now a coworker at the high school Ellie had once attended.

It had taken her a while to start calling her colleagues by their first names.

She had taught at a private school for a while, about forty-five minutes away, and then had taught at a high school in Portland before coming back to Caldwell, all the way in the desolate eastern part of the state of Oregon, where she'd decided to take a job as an English teacher at her alma mater.

Coming back to town had been . . .

Well, it was loaded. And not just because of her sister.

"Is everything all right?"

Angelica was at the top of the stairs, holding her bathrobe closed.

If she had been told in ninth grade that she would one day see her biology teacher in a bathrobe, she would've died.

"Not really. Melanie." She couldn't even bring herself to say it out loud. But she didn't want Angelica to think Melanie was dead. Which was, of course, the first thing *she* had thought when she'd seen an unfamiliar number on the phone coming through at this late hour. "I've got to go to the hospital. She . . . she had a baby."

"Oh, honey. Do you need somebody to go with you?"

"No. I just have to . . ." She closed her eyes. "I have to go."

She walked out the front door to the curb where she'd parked her little sedan. She got inside and took a deep breath as she gripped the steering wheel. She didn't know what she was going to do. At least the school year had ended last week. A bubble of laughter escaped her lips. Hysteria, really.

But she still had no idea what she was going to do, and the words of the social worker who had called her were echoing in her head.

Temporary placement. Emergency care.

A baby girl.

The hospital was fifteen minutes away, and she was just barely holding it together. What if this had happened somewhere else? Melanie and Ty weren't always in town. Ellie was a little surprised she hadn't known Melanie was pregnant. Of course, her parents wouldn't know. They'd given up on Melanie a long time ago. There was a reason the hospital had contacted Ellie.

She could freak out later. She needed to get there. She needed to figure out exactly what was going on. She needed . . .

She would cry later. Later, Ellie was going to sob her heart out.

But not now. She just needed to get through the next couple of hours.

She pulled up to the maternity ward at the hospital and parked before heading into the facility.

She paused at the front desk.

"Who are you here to see?"

She did not answer that question. Melanie Parks wasn't the person who'd called her. She was here to see the baby. She was here to see a social worker. Someone from Child Protective Services.

"I got a call from CPS," she said.

"Oh," the woman said. "You can just put CPS."

"Thank you," she said, her throat tight.

She leaned in and put her name, then CPS, followed by the date and time on the sign-in sheet. And was given a name tag and sent inside.

"You can come into the room," a nurse said, looking down at her name tag.

"I . . ." She hadn't seen Melanie for a year. And she was scared. She didn't know how bad her sister would look. How much difference the ravages of drugs would've made in the time since she'd last seen her.

When she walked into the hospital room, the curtain was shut.

"Visitor," the nurse said.

The curtain swept open, and her heart jumped. But her sister wasn't there. Neither was her sister's longtime boyfriend, Ty Porter, whom Melanie blamed for absolutely everything. Instead, she found herself staring at the tall, broad frame of a cowboy, his back to her, cradling a baby.

He didn't even have to turn around for her to know who it was.

Clark Porter.

"I . . ."

He turned around, and her heart leapt up into the center of her throat. Goddamn Clark Porter. She should hate the Porters. Really, she did.

But Clark had always been a tall, disastrous drink of whiskey that she knew she couldn't afford to take.

He had gotten here before her.

It was an echo of about a hundred other moments in their lives. Whether it was a rent-by-the-hour motel parking lot. An ER. The parking lot of a Wendy's. All those times they'd responded to SOS calls from their siblings and shown up ready to do battle for them.

And often with each other.

Clark was someone she saw much more often than she wanted to. It was always a crisis. And when she saw him, her body went into fight-or-flight response—her stomach going tight, her heart beating hard and heavy.

Fitting this time, because this was inarguably a crisis.

"What are you doing here?"

"Ty called me," he said, his voice rough.

"Child services called me," she said, and she felt her tone sounded petulant, more wounded than she intended it to.

"We should both take that meeting," he said.

She shook her head, not understanding fully. "Why?"

"They're looking for family to take her."

"Yes, and I assume they were going to ask me."

She felt strangled by the circumstances. She didn't think she was in a place to take care of a baby, but she wasn't a homeless drug addict, so she was definitely a more stable option than her sister.

"They signed over their rights," Clark said.

"They did?"

The wave of grief was fresh and overwhelming.

Melanie had a baby. Melanie wasn't even going to try to raise the baby. In many ways, it was a shocking, definitive act of love on her sister's part, but Ellie couldn't help feeling broken by it. That her sister was choosing drugs over her baby.

It isn't that simple. You know it's not. She isn't going to bring this child into that chaotic ocean of her life and let her drown along with them.

"The social worker can speak to you both, if you like," the nurse said.

"Yeah," Clark said, nodding.

Ellie was transfixed then by the little bundle in his arms. Tiny and pink, scrunched up in that tightly wrapped blanket. She had a little cap on her head, and she was just . . . perfect.

"Has there been . . . medically . . ."

"She's good," Clark said.

They were now standing there alone in the room. She could clearly remember the last time she'd seen Clark. She'd been horrible, actually, and she felt bad about it, but not bad enough to apologize. Not even now, a year later.

Yeah, it had been about a year.

A year since she'd seen Clark, and Ty, and Melanie. They'd been in a motel parking lot, Ty and Melanie having a huge fight, the motel owner threatening to call the police.

Just come with me, Mel.

I can't!

Of course she couldn't, because Ellie wouldn't enable her drug use. Of course she couldn't, because even when they were monsters to each other, she and Ty were in the kind of toxic love written about in bad teen romances.

When Ty and Melanie had driven off and left her there with the angry motel owner and Clark, she'd lost it at him.

He'd paid the motel bill.

That still bothered her. They should have split it.

"She doesn't have . . . They don't think she has any issues from . . . You know that Melanie had to have been on drugs."

Ellie was almost positive Melanie hadn't been sober for more than thirty days in the last ten years. She hadn't kept in close contact with her sister, but if Melanie had managed any extended sobriety, she would have told Ellie.

"The baby's perfectly healthy. I'm sure there are things that might come up later, things they can't look for now, but she doesn't have any obvious problems."

The relief she felt was extreme. "Thank God. Did you know?"

He shook his head. "No. I didn't know. Ty called me right after she was born. Said there was no way they could look after her, and that he needed me to come and get her."

"I must be on some form that Melanie filled out," she said. She didn't have a way of getting in touch with her sister. Melanie was more likely to have a burner phone than anything else.

"I'll take her," she said.

"You're not just going to take her, Ellie. She's my niece, just the same as yours. And I want to take care of her."

"Clark," she said, his name coming out of her mouth in a rush, tasting strange on her tongue. Of all the weird things about this moment, she didn't need to go getting tangled up about Clark. "Your lifestyle is not conducive to raising a baby."

"I'm retired from the rodeo. Didn't you know?"

"Oh. I guess you must've taken me off your Christmas card list."

"Funny. I just figured, in a small town, news travels quickly. I knew that you were back teaching at the high school."

"Probably because my mom was bragging about it."

She knew that, in general, her mother wasn't completely happy with her decision to become a teacher. But considering her other child was a homeless drug addict, Nancy Parks was going to be bragging about that teaching job.

"Could be. And you know my mom wasn't bragging about me."

Because his mom was face down in a pool of her own problems, her own addictions, and probably not paying attention to the one functional child she had.

It was a double-edged sword, Ellie knew.

They were from different sorts of dysfunction, but the Parks family at least had a genteel sort of dysfunction to it.

Well, until Melanie. She'd taken quiet dysfunction and turned it into something loud.

"I'm retired," he reiterated. "And my house has just been finished. I'm starting up a ranch on the outskirts of town. I'm in a great position to take this on."

"Do you have . . . Are you with somebody?"

"No. What does that have to do with anything?"

"It just seems like a weird thing to me. That a single man would voluntarily curb his . . . I don't know, his game?" Which was maybe what her students would call it. Or maybe not. She was always a little bit behind on the slang. And they were happy to point it out to her.

"I sowed all the wild oats I need to. I traveled with the rodeo for fifteen years. I'm done with that. I have all the money I need, and I'm just settling in to have a more normal life."

"I'm planning on buying a house in about eight months," she said.

"Good. You're also going to be working full time away from home."

"I don't have work in the summer."

He looked down at the little girl in his arms, and then there was a knock at the door. "Hello," came a soft voice. A woman with dark curly hair and dark, soulful eyes came in. Her entire demeanor was calm. Empathetic.

The exact sort of demeanor you wanted in a school counselor or a child services worker, she figured.

"Hi," she and Clark said at the same time.

"My name is Daisy Lynnfield. I am a social worker. I was here when your sister and her partner relinquished their parental rights.

They also said that they had close family who could take their child."

"Me," Ellie said. "I'm her sister. I'm a teacher. I . . ."

Daisy nodded. "Yes. Melanie did mention that she had a sister. But Ty also mentioned a brother."

"That's me," said Clark. "We're both financially able to take care of a baby. And in very different places in our lives."

She appreciated that Clark hadn't tried to push himself out in front of her.

"It's completely understandable if neither of you is prepared to take this on now. We can find temporary placement for the baby until we can make some decisions."

Ellie tried to imagine that tiny baby in Clark's arms going into the home of a stranger.

What if they didn't get her back? What if they never saw her again? She didn't know enough about the system. Obviously, she'd taught kids over the years who were in care, but she always had the sense that the system was underfunded, understaffed, and overcrowded. The idea of this little girl being caught in that impersonal, imperfect system terrified her.

And God knew what would happen. This social worker couldn't guarantee her safety. There would already be so much . . . so much trauma baked into that little body. Who knew how stressed Melanie had been during the pregnancy. Whether she'd been on drugs or having withdrawals from them at different times. Where they'd been sleeping, what sort of care she'd gotten.

"No. That won't be necessary."

"I could take her now," Clark said. "I mean, I'll have to get a car seat."

"We can help with that," the social worker said.

"I want to take her," Ellie said.

"You said you were getting a house in eight months, Ellie. What kind of living situation are you in right now?"

She wanted to punch Clark for questioning her. She was responsible, and she always had been. Always. Even all the way back in high school, and he knew that. To question her, as if she might not have all her ducks in a row, as if she might bring their niece into a bad situation, was just obnoxious.

"I'm rooming with Mrs. C.," she said, knowing that would shock and horrify him.

His face contorted. "Seriously? The biology teacher?"

"Yes. I'm surprised you paid attention."

"Just enough to graduate," he said.

"So you two know each other," the social worker said.

"Yes. We both grew up here," Ellie said. "And our siblings have been . . ." She sighed heavily. "They've been together since high school. Toxic and together, in active addiction pretty much since they were sixteen. We're their . . ."

"We're the emergency contacts," Clark said.

That they were. "So yeah," she said. "We know each other."

"I don't think there's any reason that we have to choose," Clark said. "We can share custody. Like divorced parents, right?"

"In Oregon, yes. Particularly in cases of kinship adoption. If you want to adopt."

"Yes," they both said together.

"The field will be clear for that," Daisy said. "The parents have relinquished their rights, and both of them said that they wanted you to be involved."

"Is there a birth certificate or . . ."

"Yes, but in the event of adoption, both of your names can go on it."

She and Clark looked at each other. His steely blue gaze was hard, but determined.

Was she really going to do this? Were they going to adopt this baby? No thought had gone into the decision. And if it was any other situation, she would've said no. She wasn't prepared to be a mother. The idea wasn't even on her radar. She hadn't been in a relationship in at least three years. She'd been focusing on teaching. On getting her life in order. She was a ducks-in-a row kind of person. Probably a side effect of being the older sibling of a sister who was constantly on the verge of crashing out. But there was no choice here. This baby was their niece. And they were both from dysfunctional families. The families that had created Ty and Melanie.

She and Clark had their lives together. As much as she wanted to be harsh on him because of his family history, she had to admit that he was doing well.

But doing this with him? That meant submitting herself to a constant feeling of fight or flight. The constant stomach-tensing, heart-palpitating Clark of it all.

You'll get used to it. For her.

"This is what we want," she said. "We want to adopt her."

"Then we'll work with you to make that happen."

Chapter 2

God Almighty, how had he gotten himself into this? Clark asked himself for the hundredth time as the car seat was fitted into his truck.

This was bad in about a hundred different ways, and here he was, doing it anyway.

He had no idea what to do with a baby.

And he'd never known what the hell to do with Ellie Parks.

In truth, he knew now, as he'd always done, exactly what he wanted to do with Ellie. From the moment he'd first met her, he'd wanted to kiss her senseless. But he'd been Clark Porter from the wrong side of the tracks, and she was Ellie Parks, from the nicest gated community in town, and there was just no way she'd have ever looked twice at him.

Unfortunately for everyone, her younger sister had done more than look twice at Clark's younger brother, Ty.

So had begun the fifteen-year hell of that toxic relationship descending into addiction, and all the reasons Ellie had been off-limits back then were even more complicated now.

Now their siblings had thrown a baby right into the mix.

He could've walked away. He could've left the baby with Ellie, and that might've been the more virtuous thing by a mile. But the minute he'd seen her, that little squirt, lying in the bassinet, abandoned by both of her parents, he'd known that she was his.

His *responsibility*, if nothing more.

He'd never been able to help his little brother straighten his life out. Ty had been hell in cowboy boots from the moment he was born, and what had been cute for a long time had turned into something reckless and dangerous, and he'd taken Melanie down with him.

Now Clark was responsible for this little girl. And bringing her home with him. At two in the morning.

The hospital had stocked them up with things like diapers, formula, bottles, and some extra onesies. And Ellie was going to follow him back to his place.

"God Almighty," he muttered again as he got into the truck. "Just follow me," he said before closing the truck door.

Ellie disappeared from view, and a few moments later, a small sedan emerged from a parking space, and he pulled out in front of her, making sure to signal as he left the parking lot so that she could follow him.

He was exhausted. And completely lost in thought on the way back home. So much so that he almost missed the turnoff to his own driveway. He put his blinker on quickly and cranked the wheel, with the car behind him making the same abrupt maneuver. She was going to be mad at him about that.

This outcome felt right, almost, as much as it felt wrong and broken. His new house was finished. Now he felt like there was a purpose to it. Like this place existed for her.

For that little baby. Who needed a name.

He pulled up to the front of the house and turned the truck off slowly.

Then he opened the driver's side door. By the time he got around the truck to open up the back and get the baby out of the car seat, Ellie was there.

"I've got her."

He nodded. He opted to gather the baby supplies, including a little bassinet that had been gifted to them by the hospital, and carry them into the house.

The place still felt so new. It was barely lived in at this point. The entryway was bright, clean. Everything was immaculate. He was proud of that.

His heart clenched tight. His brother's decision to surrender his rights made him sad. But it was also heroic. He and Ty had grown up in the middle of the hell of their parents' addictions, and his brother hadn't come out unscathed. Their parents had passed it all on to him, and the one thing he'd done to break the cycle was to make sure his own kid didn't get caught up in it.

Their parents hadn't been able to do that for them.

Clark really appreciated that his brother had done that for his daughter.

This was why he had a nice house. It was why he was clean and sober, not even indulging in so much as a beer, even though that had been unpopular on the rodeo circuit.

It was for this. Because he couldn't save Ty.

But he could save this little bundle.

That mattered.

"I don't know much about babies," Ellie said softly, unbuckling the car seat right there in the entryway, and taking the little girl out of it, cradling her in her arms.

Goddamn. Ellie had always been pretty.

But pretty was a dime a dozen. There had always been something about her that appealed to him specifically. Something that made his breath catch every time he saw her, even in moments like this when he shouldn't be thinking about her that way at all.

But it was always like this. He'd lost track of the number of times they'd shown up at the same location to bail Mel and Ty out—sometimes literally.

Ellie was a lot less angry with him this time than she normally was. But maybe he could credit the baby with that.

Harder to call him names with a child present.

And with such high stakes.

Funny, now she was rooming with their old biology teacher, and he was the one with the big fancy place.

Life had a way of changing fortunes.

He wouldn't say he felt superior, though. She was a teacher. In his life, teachers had made a difference. Whether they were his teachers in school, or mentors at the ranch where he'd worked in high school.

They were the only adults he'd had positive interactions with.

"I thought you had to have a degree in . . . *children* in order teach."

"Sure. Kids that are old enough to be in a classroom."

"Fair enough. I have a guest room."

"Right. I don't know if I can sleep. I'm exhausted but . . ."

"Yeah," he said.

She followed him into the living room, and he sat down on the couch, looking at the grand wall of windows that overlooked the valley. She sat on the love seat, a decent distance away from him, holding the baby.

"I thought they were calling to tell me Melanie was dead."

"Yeah. I kind of thought the same thing."

"Didn't your call come from Ty?"

"Yeah. He called me, but I'll admit I kind of thought maybe some cops had picked his phone up."

"You had his number."

He nodded. "I've had it. Just in case."

"Melanie doesn't keep in touch with me. I'm shocked that they were able to contact me."

"Maybe she remembered your number."

She laughed. "Well, then she opts never to call it."

"I imagine for the last nine months she's been pretty scared."

"I bet. I wonder if this was their plan all along, or if they were trying to get into a better place before the baby was born."

"I expect they wanted to do better. They're not bad people. They're just . . . broken."

"I've always blamed him."

"Fair enough. But why?"

She looked up at him. "I've always blamed your brother, but that's not really fair. Mel has a stake in her own life. Especially after all these years. At this point she has to take responsibility for her choices."

"They can't quit drugs or each other, unfortunately."

"Yeah."

She laughed, though it wasn't a very cheerful sound. "I just can't believe . . . She's had a more long-lasting relationship than any of mine. So, maybe that's what I'm missing."

"Well, God knows I don't have any romantic relationships to show for the last fifteen years."

There was nothing funny about the situation. But the truth was, you either learned to laugh, or you cried all the time.

"I'm sorry," Clark said. "That my brother got your sister tied up in all of this."

"You don't need to be sorry for that," she said. "The one thing we can do is make sure this innocent child doesn't suffer."

"That's for damn sure," he said.

"You hear that, little one?" Ellie asked. "We're going to take care of you."

He'd known when his phone rang that his whole life was about to change. He'd just had no idea how.

Now he did. Tonight he'd become a father.

CHAPTER 3

When Ellie woke up the next morning, she was groggy and disoriented.

And then everything slammed into her. Right. She'd only slept for a couple of hours because—

She sat bolt upright and looked at the bassinet that was set up right beside her bed. The baby was sleeping.

Her heart leapt, and she put her hand on the newborn's chest, felt her heart beating beneath her palm.

Then she put a hand on her own chest, feeling the erratic heartbeat there.

"Holy crap," she said. "This is going to be a long eighteen years, Baby Girl."

She reached into the bassinet and picked the baby up. A little squeak and flex of her body were the infant's only reactions.

Ellie took her phone out of her purse, which she'd dumped next to the bed, and saw that she had several texts from Angelica. Ellie had said she'd be gone all night, but hadn't gone into any details.

She pushed the microphone icon to send a voice-to-text message, and gave Angelica a download of everything that had happened as she started to get out of bed. Then she walked down the stairs, holding Baby Girl close as she followed the scent of coffee.

Clark was standing there in the kitchen, barefoot, wearing nothing but a pair of blue jeans, and her heart did a somersault. He was . . . extraordinary. His back was thickly muscled, and there was a scar on his side that piqued her interest. She wanted to examine it closely but she also wanted to run out of the room.

Was this fight or flight?

He turned to face her, and her heart did not calm down.

No. No, it wasn't panic, sadly.

He was a fine man. His chest was heavily muscled too, his abdomen ridged. He looked like the kind of guy who worked out in the gym, except she knew he didn't. It was all from riding bulls and generally being a really hot cowboy. Because of him, she had decided that cowboys weren't her type. Because of the way he made her throat dry in high school, and made her heart race, and was the subject of her very first sex dream.

Before she'd ever even had sex.

Yeah. There was simply no need for her to dwell on that. Or on the tattoo he had on his rib cage, in scrolling cursive that she couldn't read, but desperately wanted to.

Her eyes shot back up to his, her whole body tingling with the awareness that she'd been so busy looking at his torso, it was probably obvious.

"Good morning," he said, his voice rough.

"Good morning. She needs a name."

"I agree," he said. "But I don't exactly have a list of baby names on hand."

"Yeah. Me either."

Well, secretly, she'd always wanted to name a baby after her grandmother, who had been the sweetest, most soft-spoken woman, but with a steely determination. She had been kind, but never one to be taken advantage of.

"Marjorie," she said. "Our grandmother . . . Melanie had a

great relationship with her. She died when we were in middle school. I think she would like that as a name."

"Well, it's kind of an old lady name," he said. "But then, new babies look a little bit like old people."

"Agreed. On both counts. But I think it's a fine tribute. And one that she'll appreciate. Someday. Melanie, I mean."

She didn't know if Melanie was ever going to have contact with her own daughter. She couldn't really picture the future right now. Overnight their lives had changed.

She and Clark had only interacted during sibling emergencies. They saw each other in the worst, most stressful moments of their lives.

Now here she was, standing in his kitchen, holding a baby, wearing yesterday's clothes, while he stood there shirtless and barefoot.

"Marjorie Porter."

She frowned. "I don't know about that."

"Why not?"

"Because you're not adopting her by yourself."

"No. But I assume she'll be given her daddy's name."

She one hundred percent knew what he meant. But it sounded as if he was calling himself Daddy, which made her think about . . .

She shook her head. She was in a little bit of a dry spell. Okay, a lot of a dry spell. Ever since she and Jason had called it quits, she'd just kind of given up.

She wasn't a romantic. Not really. She didn't feel she could afford to be. Her independence was important to her, but she definitely hadn't imagined a future in which she was thirty-three and extremely single.

And just like that, you're an instant mother.

Well, there was a gift to her biological clock.

"What time did CPS say they were coming by today?" he asked.

"I think around nine," she said.

"I need to finish this coffee then."

"Me too," she agreed.

They caffeinated, then he whisked the baby away to change her diaper. Not long after that, Daisy showed up and interviewed them together, then took a tour of the home.

"I think this should be a very fast process," she said.

"Good," they replied in unison.

And just like that, their lives were on a completely different trajectory than what they'd imagined.

Once Daisy left, Ellie wasn't quite sure what they were supposed to do. How they were going to work all this out.

"Ellie," Clark said, "I think you're going to have to move in with me."

CHAPTER 4

He hadn't expected to make the offer. It had just sort of come out of his mouth over dinner. But there hadn't been a good time at any point in the day for her to leave. It just never felt right.

And he'd felt something burning in his chest all day. Only when the words had come out of his mouth did he realize exactly what it was.

What was he thinking? Putting himself in close proximity to this woman who made him feel so much that it pushed him right to the edge.

"What?"

"It's the only thing that makes sense. This place is huge, I have plenty of room. You're living in somebody else's house, and it's not your permanent plan anyway. You're trying to save up and move into your own place . . ."

"I'm not exactly strapped for cash. I'm saving up for a down payment."

"I get that. But you can do that here. And while Marjorie is little, we'll coparent in the same home. It just makes sense. The thing is, we're not exes. Our parenting doesn't have to be traditional in that sense. We don't have to have two different households. We can actually give her a really stable upbringing. Hell, probably more stable than either of us had, if you think about it."

It was true. He hadn't been given a whole lot of a chance to think the situation through, but it was true. There was no reason the two of them couldn't build something strong for this little girl.

"Ty and Melanie did the absolute best they could by her. And I know not everybody would understand that, but we both do. Because we know how it's been for them. All this time."

She nodded, swallowing hard. "I know."

"And now we have a chance to honor their wishes. They weren't selfish. They weren't. Yeah, I know some people would say addiction is selfish, but you and I both know it makes their lives miserable. If they could just kick it, they would."

He could see his little brother then. As he had been. Just himself. Grinning and causing mayhem, full of life, full of joy.

Drugs had taken his love of life from Ty. He was Clark's little brother but he looked older than Clark now.

"I know what you're saying, but it just seems like . . . We don't know each other very well, and we've never particularly gotten along . . ."

"You're talking about the time you yelled at me for being a goddamn Porter who broke up your family?"

She scrunched her face up. "Did I say that?"

"You did indeed. You were pretty angry. We were paying to get their car out of the impound."

"Yeah. I know. I try not think about it."

"It's hard, and because your parents washed their hands of—"

"Yes, thank you," she snapped. "I don't actually need a reminder of what my parents did."

"Hey, at least your parents have a right to be disappointed. Mine kind of created the problem."

She made a face that he couldn't quite decode.

"I don't know that I agree with that. My parents caused some issues. It just wasn't exactly the same. I mean, I know that you guys had it worse. Rougher than we did."

"That's almost an olive branch," he said.

"That doesn't mean I forgive your brother. Or that I'm not angry at him. I'm just saying I understand that you guys grew up in a house where there was a lot of addiction."

"That we did," Clark said. "But I'm certainly not going to defend him. Not at this point."

They both looked at the little baby. "I do think giving her up was the best thing Melanie and Ty could've done," Ellie said.

And the best thing she and Clark could do was to come together and try to raise the baby as a unit.

"When it comes to figuring out how to raise a kid, I assume your family's a lot more functional than mine."

She grimaced. "In my family, love is conditional. There's a lot of pressure. From my mother. My dad works. He earns money, and I think in his mind that's the sum of his obligation to the family. Whenever I go over, Dad is just sitting in his chair, watching sports, doing his own thing. When he's not working, he's watching the Bill Parks show. To compensate, I guess my mom was kind of a helicopter parent. But not in a super-loving way. In a way that we felt she was disappointed in us all the time."

"Sounds like a sitcom," he said.

"I guess it would."

"It's no secret that my parents have struggled. I mean, it's basically in the local news every so often."

"Not you," she said, looking around at the house. "This is . . . It's more than a little bit impressive."

"Thanks."

God. What he wouldn't have given for her to notice him back all those years ago. It was a trip. She hadn't been snobby, not exactly. There had been an untouchable air about her, and he'd known better than to go there.

His brother, not so much.

And it had resulted in disaster.

Now . . . they needed to band together to raise their niece.

Caring for little Marjorie was the most important thing. Attraction to Ellie had no place in that.

What a dumbass thought to entertain even for a moment. In fact, it was so stupid that he wasn't going to put words to it. He was just going to push it to the side.

They'd been given a brief overview of the adoption process, and truly, in their case, it seemed straightforward. Oregon made it pretty easy for nontraditional families to adopt, and Ty and Melanie had voluntarily surrendered their parental rights, naming their siblings as the preferred adoptive parents.

But that was just the legal stuff. There was also the practical, personal stuff.

"Do you really want me to move in?"

"I have plenty of room. I have five bedrooms here. We can put the nursery in between our rooms, and we can take care of her together. I think that would be the best thing."

She looked hesitant. "We don't know each other very well."

"I guess not. But how well do you know our old biology teacher?"

"She is my coworker."

"Sure. And I'm your old classmate."

"Probably also my common-law brother-in-law at this point?"

He laughed. "Is that a thing?"

"I think it's a thing when you end up raising your niece."

She let out a low sound. "I am going to have to tell my mother. And I'm really not looking forward to it."

"What worries you?" he asked, leaning against the counter and looking at her.

"That she won't want to be involved. Or worse, that she will. That worries me. It worries me pretty substantially. Because she's difficult, and she's going to be handsy, and . . ."

"You don't think that she's going to want to adopt Marjorie?"

Ellie laughed. "No. I think she might want to performatively grandparent, but I don't think she would ever want to adopt her. It would hinder her too much. And she doesn't ever like to be inconvenienced. I don't know."

"My parents will probably be happy," he said.

There was a heaviness that came along with that realization. They would be. They loved their kids, in their way. It was just that nothing in their lives was conducive to taking care of children. It didn't mean that they didn't care; it just meant that their priorities were all mixed up.

They were kind of like Ty and Melanie, honestly.

He wasn't sure about his own priorities. He'd achieved financial success. But he wasn't married. Had never had a serious relationship.

He liked sex, sure. A little entanglement could be fun, especially when he was out on the road. But anything beyond that . . .

The weight of responsibility always felt like it was a little bit too much.

And now he had a whole kid.

Jumping right into the deep end. Maybe not being an addict wasn't enough to be a good parent. Maybe he wouldn't be able to sort his priorities out because he hadn't been raised to know what they should be.

"I really need you to move in," he said. "Because at least you know what a family is supposed to look like. I don't. I built this house, but I'm not even sure what I did it for. Except that it looked right. It's like a TV set, isn't it? Perfect and just so, but with no real life to it. I don't know anything about being part of a family. Maybe between the two of us, we can figure it out."

CHAPTER 5

For Ellie, today *figuring it out* took the form of talking to Angelica about moving out within the week—Angelica didn't mind at all; the arrangement had never been intended to be long-term—and going to the store to pick up some supplies for Marjorie.

Clark wanted to go to a big-box store about a half hour away, while she wanted to visit some of the boutiques in town.

The trouble with small towns was there was no way they were going to be able to keep people from asking questions.

The main street had changed significantly in the last few years. A revival of people supporting local shops and restaurants instead of chain stores meant that there were new boutiques popping up all the time. Sometimes they didn't last. Getting business right in a town this size was difficult.

But it also meant that a lot of the shop owners were people who were new to town, strangers to both Ellie and Clark, and honestly, that suited her just fine.

Main Street was dotted with statues. A majestic bald eagle, a pioneer woman. A shirtless cowboy who—though she was loath to admit it—reminded her a little bit of Clark. The image of him shirtless yesterday was still on her mind.

She tried to ignore that thought as they continued down the street, with Clark holding Marjorie and Ellie taking the lead.

The baby was so tiny in his arms. And she really couldn't look at him holding her for too long, because it made a whole chain reaction go off inside her. An unsuspected hormonal response that was heretofore unknown to her, suddenly cascading through her body.

Bodies were like that. Susceptible to biological imperatives and whatever else.

She didn't need to be a science teacher to know that.

When they walked into the first boutique, she felt as if her chest might cave in. Everything inside it was so tiny and cute. The pink, frilly little outfits sent a rush through her. Oh God. Where was all this coming from? She'd been perfectly happy to wait to have kids and . . .

She felt guilty. Guilty that she was having this moment when her sister wasn't. Guilty that her sister's baby was fulfilling something inside her when . . .

"Are you okay?"

Oh, now he was being nice.

"I'm fine," she said.

"Welcome in," said a smiling woman behind the counter. She had big blond curls and a T-shirt that was knotted up beneath her breasts, a long, high-waisted skirt with a loud geometric pattern swirling around her legs.

"Thank you," Ellie said.

"Aren't you just the cutest couple. And what a sweet baby."

She and Clark looked at each other, mutually wondering if this was going to be their life. Every parent-teacher conference. Every holiday, every event. People were going to wonder what the connection between them was.

And without getting into the messy family history, there was no way to neatly explain who they were to each other.

Especially not now, when they were adopting Marjorie. They were going to be her parents. So she just smiled, and so did Clark.

"She's a fresh one," the lady said.

"Yes," Ellie said, "and we need pretty much everything."

"Really? No baby shower?"

Yes. Small-town shopping. She should have anticipated that even if she didn't know the shopkeeper, it was going to be weird.

"We . . . adopted her. Or we are adopting her. She was placed with us just a couple of days ago. So it's a surprise."

"Oh," the woman said, her eyes filling with tears. "That's so lovely of you both."

Ellie felt as if she was walking in a minefield.

"We think we're the lucky ones," Clark said.

Knowing the situation, the actual situation, Ellie knew that it was more complicated than that. She also knew that Marjorie was going to grow up hearing reactions like this. That she was lucky. And why? She wasn't a burden. And she and Clark weren't saintly for taking her in. She was a little girl who needed a home. Clark had a home. And Ellie would have one, as well. They had love they could give her. Why wouldn't they do that? But that didn't make them special any more than it made Marjorie lucky to have them.

Clark was exactly right. Ellie felt lucky. Even though her life had been derailed, completely different today from what it had been two days ago, she felt lucky.

That feeling intensified as she looked at the clothes.

Clark put a hand on her elbow, and she tried not to flinch. "I don't know how to say this delicately, but there's no budget."

She looked at him. Right. So he didn't have any money because he'd just finished building the house. That made sense. "I don't mind buying the clothes. I have some savings from my down payment fund, and I don't mind pulling from it, especially not since—"

"No," he said. "You don't understand. There is no limit to the budget. You can get whatever you want."

She could only stare at him. "What?"

"I've done very well for myself," he said, keeping his voice low. "Between my winnings, my investments, and my endorsement deals, I'm set."

"I don't . . . I don't fully understand that."

"You don't have to. Just know that I'm going to buy everything, and you don't need to look at the price tag."

Never in her life had that been a thing. And here she was now, on a pink shopping spree with the cutest baby she'd ever seen, and a gorgeous cowboy in tow. If it didn't feel so unreal, she would be in awe. It was too bad there was so much going on beneath the surface.

She decided not to dwell on the complications.

She chose dresses, onesies, little jackets and socks, and a beautiful, very expensive stroller. They carried the spoils back to the truck, and then Marjorie went into the stroller as they continued down the street.

In each shop, people commented on how beautiful their family was, and Ellie started really listening to the reactions people had when they found out she and Clark had adopted Marjorie.

"This feels really complicated," she said when they went back to the truck later.

"In what way?"

"I feel so . . . happy to have Marjorie. No, this isn't what I planned. And it's a total direction shift. But when I think about her, having her, raising her as time goes on, I feel a sense of real joy. But then I stop myself from feeling it because our joy is built off Melanie and Ty's pain. But I don't want Marjorie to live in their world. You've seen how people react when we say we adopted her. They act like we are saints. Like she's some kind of a burden. And that's just not true or fair. I don't want her to get lost in the sadness of her birth parents' addiction. Because her life doesn't need to be defined by that. Honestly, that's why Melanie and Ty gave her up. To keep her from being defined by this thing they can't escape."

He nodded. "I agree."

"I want to be honest with her. I don't want to have secrets."

They got back into the truck after Clark secured Marjorie in her seat.

"I know you had a different experience growing up than I did. But one of the things I learned watching my sister descend into drug addiction is that secrets, and the things people are afraid to say, always make it worse. My parents suspected that she was drinking, engaging in substance abuse, having sex with Ty, but they were afraid to ask. Just like they were afraid to ask about anything to do with mental health. They acted as if it would all be better if we just covered it up. And I think if we had faced the truth head-on back then, things would've been better."

"We?"

"I include myself in that. What if I had said something to Melanie? What if I had been honest? What if I had confronted her when I started to suspect she was using? I'm her older sister. But I was afraid the answer would be yes. I was afraid she would already be too far gone, and because I couldn't face what she was doing, I lost her. I want everything out in the open now. I want Marjorie to know that we adopted her. That we're just a different sort of family, but a family all the same. And I want her to know that her biological parents made a very hard, very unselfish decision. Because they did."

"Yeah," he said, his voice rough. "They did."

"And I just don't want . . . The idea that we did her a favor, I want that to go away as quickly as possible."

She felt extremely protective. And angry that anyone would treat their beautiful baby like a burden.

"We're her mom and dad," she said, the words coming out of her mouth before she fully thought them through.

"Yeah," he said.

"It's a little overwhelming but it's also amazing. Two days ago, we didn't really have a connection at all, and now this little soul is transforming our lives."

"No connection besides dysfunction, I guess," he said, though there was a note in his voice that she couldn't quite decode.

They brought their purchases back to the house, and it felt good to put everything away. They still had to order certain things. There was just a plain dark cherry dresser in the room for now, but some cute, baby-appropriate furniture was on the way—pieces in brighter colors, that were a little bit more whimsical, and a rocking chair.

Marjorie fussed for a while, clearly filled with opinions about how strenuous the day had been.

And Ellie couldn't blame her. She spent some time getting the baby settled for a nap with their brand-new baby monitor set out so that she could take it down the stairs and not lose touch with her tiny charge.

By the time she went into the kitchen, Clark was cooking.

"Are you making dinner?"

"Yes, I am."

"I didn't realize that you . . . cooked."

"Funny thing. I eat. So it makes a lot of sense for me to have that skill."

"Sure," she said. "But you're a rodeo cowboy who also claims to have limitless funds. I guess I thought that maybe you . . . I dunno, didn't cook for yourself."

"I'm also a control freak," he said. He looked at her, and she didn't think she was imagining that his grin was a little bit wicked. She curled her fingers into fists and ignored her body's response. Ignored the heat that engulfed her.

Yes. Clark Porter was hot. He always had been.

What he hadn't always been was her coparent.

During the last fifteen years, he would have been a bad decision for any number of reasons. But now he was much more than a potential bad decision. Now he was off-limits because the stakes were way too high.

Also, she was Ellie Parks.

And the thing about that was . . . she was boring. In high

school, Clark had always dated flashy girls. She had no idea what kind of women he'd been dating since then, but he was an incredibly hot, wildly successful rodeo cowboy, and that implied a few different things.

He probably had a lot more experience than she, and a lot more skill.

Also, she had no business thinking about it.

"I realize that we know each other superficially. But we don't know much about each other," she said. His retirement and the revelation about his wealth had really driven that point home.

"True," he said. "You know me just well enough to yell at me in parking lots."

She winced. "I'm sorry about that."

The room smelled of rosemary, garlic, and butter. And when he placed the steaks in the cast-iron pan, searing them, her stomach growled.

He opened the oven, placed the skillet inside, then leaned against the counter, turning to face her. "I left here, got into the rodeo, lucked into a lot of success there."

"Were you ever tempted to start using? Like your parents. Like Ty."

"No, because it's a dead end. I could see it then, just like I see it now. I always figured that I couldn't let my parents' behavior determine how far I was going to get in life. Bottom line, I just really didn't want to be like them. I thought I could do better, and so I did better. The end."

"It's not that simple, though, is it? You have to have drive and direction and confidence to succeed."

Clark shrugged. "Ty and I are different. We always have been. He was always a risk-taker. And I know that people would look at what I do in the rodeo and assume the same about me. But it's not the same. I don't have a death wish. I care about my life. I care about what happens to me. I always had the sense that Ty never liked himself. That if he drove too fast and hit a tree, he would die with an adrenaline rush and that would be good enough for him.

I never wanted to die. I also didn't want to live the way they do. I saw the rodeo as a way out. I didn't do it because I needed the thrill, but it was something I was good at. I started working at one of the ranches on the outskirts of town when I was . . . fourteen, I guess, and I did that all the way through school. I learned how to be a cowboy. I think that's the thing. I had something I cared about. I had an identity. I don't think Ty had that. Which meant he was happy to surrender himself to drugs and hope they'd make him into somebody. But that was just never me. It was never what I wanted."

"That's incredible," she said. And she meant it. "I'd love to have you come and talk to the kids in my class."

"Me?"

"Yes. Because I think what you just said . . . I wish more people knew it when they were teenagers. You've got to have things to live for. I wonder if that was Melanie's problem. She knew what our parents wanted for her. And she didn't want it."

"What did they want?"

"Melanie was a ballerina," she said. "She was so pretty when she danced. It was so important to my mom, but there was a point where I think it wasn't important to Melanie anymore. More than that, it was a burden. I think being with Ty felt like an escape. And drugs were like an express train right out of that future. She didn't want the pressure anymore. And I get it. But I wish she'd found another outlet for herself. I wish she'd known what she wanted."

His eyes were assessing, and she felt something stir in her chest. "What about you? What made you decide to be a teacher?"

"I wanted the chance to reach even one kid like my sister. To be there to ask the right questions, which I didn't do with her. To . . ." She closed her eyes. "I think it's important. I think teenagers are brilliant and bright and vulnerable. They make these huge, life-altering decisions about their bodies and their futures, and their frontal lobes aren't even fully developed. And I just . . . I care. It's really hard sometimes."

"Yeah, I can't remember being too nice to any of my teachers. Seems like a thankless job."

"No. I wouldn't say that."

"But do you do it for you? Or is it just for her?"

His question was insightful. "Yes," she said. "I do it for me."

"For more than just your guilt?"

She laughed. "Yes. I like English. I have an English degree. You have to do something with it."

He laughed. "Well, money isn't really your number one objective, then."

She shook her head. "No. It's not. Partly because . . . I grew up in a house with plenty of it. But money didn't fix everything. Growing up the way that you did is hard. But . . ."

"Middle ground would be nice," he said.

"Yeah. Middle ground would be great. Enough money. Enough love. What a concept."

"I think we're going to do pretty well."

"Well, I need to pack my stuff up so that we can get it all moved in."

"Guess that's a project for tomorrow," he said.

"I guess so. One step at a time."

CHAPTER 6

Well. He was moving her into his house. So that was happening.

Not into his room. Not into his bed.

He shouldn't have even had that thought.

His stomach was tight as he helped her load boxes in the back of his truck, boxes she had packed quickly, because she didn't really have any furniture and was only coming with clothes and a few items of memorabilia.

He walked back into the house and made eye contact with Mrs. C. Just looking at her made him feel as if he had missed the deadline on something. He didn't know why the hell she still had the power to make him feel that way. He hadn't cared about biology when he was in her classroom.

"I haven't seen you in years," she said, smiling at him.

"Yeah," he said, because he wasn't sure what to say to that. It wasn't like he was going to hang around the high school. He wasn't a teacher like Ellie.

"I followed a little bit of your rodeo career, Clark, believe it or not. You've done incredibly well for yourself."

He still didn't know how to take compliments like that. Not

that he heard them so often. Sure, he had fans, but for the most part people in town still saw him as a product of his family, and it was unusual for anyone who had known him in high school to say something complimentary.

He didn't know what it would take for him to feel accomplished.

He didn't lack confidence.

Not in general. But he still felt like the bottom of the barrel in a lot of ways.

Definitely not the kind of man who ought to have Ellie moving in with him.

It was funny, because she'd been so high above him back then. He didn't know what he'd thought she would do, but choosing an occupation so mundane as a teacher definitely wasn't it. She seemed like an untouchable little rich girl to him.

Soft and enticing, something he wanted in spite of himself.

He was arguably now the one with more status. Rich and in some circles famous, but his childhood feelings of inferiority didn't go away. They clung to him like ropes he couldn't quite get free of.

It was a helluva thing, that he could be a champion and still have the feeling that he wasn't quite good enough.

He really hated that. Good enough. What the hell did that even mean? And who was he trying to impress?

He supposed he could blame it on childhood trauma and growing up in a small town and all of that stuff.

He'd actually done some therapy in the last few years.

And thank God, because if he hadn't, he wouldn't be prepared for this. To be a father.

"It's great that Marjorie has the two of you," Mrs. C. said when Ellie came back down the stairs.

"It's good that we have her," he said.

"Agreed," Ellie said.

They looked at each other and smiled, because they'd already seamlessly done what they'd agreed to do. Coparenting at its finest. Hell, they both had married parents who didn't seem to coordinate that well with each other.

He hadn't lived with another person . . . in a long time. For years he'd basically lived out of a motel, and he'd been mostly by himself.

So as they headed back toward the homestead, he was overcome by a sense of strangeness.

He was shacking up with Ellie Parks, and he'd still never even touched her, never kissed her the way he used to fantasize about doing in high school.

She still got to him. Still made him burn for things he couldn't quite have.

They started bringing the boxes up to her bedroom. It didn't take long.

"I really do need to call my mom," she said, looking around the room.

"Do you?"

"Yes," she said slowly. "I'm not . . . not in regular contact with her. Talking to her is always difficult and so is she, and . . . I feel very protective of Marjorie. I'm worried that my mom is going to say something messed up that we can't come back from."

"If that happens, then at least we are liberated from having to keep in touch with her."

"I guess."

He wanted to move closer to her, wanted to hold her face. Wanted to comfort her, but he had to ask himself if that was actually a selfless inclination. Or did he just want to put his hands on her?

He knew the answer. He just wanted to touch her. Finally.

"Why do you think she's going to have a negative response?"

"I don't know. Because she's going to say something messed up about your family."

"Don't you kind of say messed-up stuff to me about that all the time?"

She looked as if she was ready to swallow her tongue. "Well. I guess, I have said . . . I'm sorry." She shook her head.

"You don't have to apologize," he said. He took a deep breath. "In all honesty, you are right. Ty did lead Melanie into addiction. And if I were you, I think I would be angry about that forever."

"There's no room for anger. Not now. Not when we have Marjorie. We need to have as much love as possible, which means we don't have time for all that."

"I didn't realize that emotions could be scheduled," he said.

"That sounds dangerously close to being therapy adjacent."

"Oh, it's not really therapy adjacent. It's straight from therapy."

She looked surprised. "You don't seem like the type."

"Why? Because I'm a rural dude who works with his hands?"

"Yeah. But also because of other things I've observed about you that are specific to you."

Something hot spiked in his gut. Maybe it wasn't fair, but he found himself being irritated. Because she didn't know him. She never had. She didn't know how he dealt with his feelings about his family.

Hell, emotion had to go somewhere.

For Ty, it was wadded up into a tight ball, shoved into the very center of his chest, and lit on fire by the drugs flowing through his veins.

Since Clark had embraced radical sobriety, it meant dealing with things in a whole different manner.

"I've been to therapy," he said. "Extensively. To deal with the trauma of growing up in my family, to get to the root of the addictive behavior that seems to run in my DNA. I don't drink. I don't do drugs. So I had to work on sorting things out instead. And I have, Ellie. Whatever you think about cowboys or poor kids or—"

"What are you saying?" She looked offended. "First of all, I'm a teacher. I have kids of every background come into my classroom, and I love each and every one of them."

"Do you make assumptions about them based on where they're from? How they dress?"

"No," she said. "Well. Maybe. But it's not about making assumptions, it's about trying to figure out where I think they might need a lift. But one of the things I also understand, Clark, is that kids who look like they come from the nicest house on the block might also be facing challenges. Sometimes the suffering happening inside a house is invisible."

"I didn't say you had it easy. But I don't like that it shocks you that I cook, that I have the emotional maturity to take a look at my own issues and decide to deal with them."

"It's not about you. It's about every . . . every relationship in my life, honestly. Clark, my parents have never dealt with a single issue. My father buries himself in work, hides away in his own hobbies and activities when he gets home. My mom needs everything around her to be perfect so that she can feel perfect. She defines herself by her house. By what her kids are doing. My sister drowned under all that pressure. She couldn't cope with the emotions overflowing inside her when she was trying to succeed at ballet. My mother drowned her spark, her talent, her personality. Everything."

She shook her head. "And then there was my boyfriend, Jason, who had the emotional intelligence of a turnip. He played Xbox instead of ever having a conversation. He was a successful man. With a good job. And I looked around the house we shared and realized I was in a younger version of my parents' marriage. Not even the promise of a commitment or children or anything like that, but with a man who worked, made the money, and then completely checked out at the end of the day. So it isn't you. I have a hard time believing that anyone around me has done the work of analyzing their emotions. I'm sorry if my surprise felt personal. If it's personal to anyone, it's me."

He felt as if little shards of glass had scattered from her lips and stuck themselves around his heart. He felt like shit, because he had just accused her unfairly, based on his own assumptions about her. Based on the way he'd felt about her in high school, and dammit, the way she still made him feel. She made him feel he wasn't good enough. She made him feel like that teenage boy who wanted nothing more than to kiss those rich-girl lips, to experience something he knew full well was too good for him.

He had brought his bullshit to her door, and all the while he'd been accusing her of doing the same thing.

"Sorry," he said. "Genuinely. That was kind of an Uno reverse."

"What?"

"You know, the game. Uno."

"No . . ."

He sighed. "Never mind. I mean that I tend to think you don't have a very high opinion of me, but that assumption is actually me not thinking very highly of you."

She looked away. "Yeah, but I've also said some really unkind things to you. So maybe be a little bit more gracious to yourself. I've never seen you do anything that wasn't kind, Clark. You've always been there for your brother. Sometimes, I just feel so angry about everything that happened to our siblings that I'm not rational."

"You don't need to be, do you?"

"I don't know. Maybe. Maybe not."

"You're the only other person I know who's been through something like this," he said. They had spent the same number of years trying to pull their siblings back from the brink. Feeling helpless to do anything about it, battling the apathy of their parents.

They had been the rescue squad. They'd been the biggest advocates for those people they loved so much, who couldn't quite escape the clutches of their awful addiction.

"I guess that's true," she said. "We had this in common the whole time, and I've been turning you into an enemy. You're not your brother. And you're not Melanie. That's the problem. I'm so angry at her, Clark. And there's nothing I can do about that. Because if I tell her how angry I am, I'm going to alienate her. More than she already is. So I've lashed out at you, because you're the easiest target. I've held on to anger at your family, but the person who's really responsible for Melanie's behavior is my sister."

"You're right. I get it. We can't even be mad at them. Not openly. And that's the hardest thing. I know it kills me. I don't want to push my brother away. I really don't. I also can't enable him."

"Yeah," she said. "It's an impossible situation. Thankless. Everybody has an opinion about how they would deal with the problem, but they don't know."

"Hell, I don't even know from one day to the next. Sometimes I think I should stop talking to Ty. Sometimes I think that any contact is enabling. But if we hadn't kept the line of communication open, I really don't think we would have Marjorie now."

"No," she said softly, moving forward and putting her hand out. Her fingers brushed his, and his heart went sharp. She looked up at him, their eyes clashing, and then she removed her hand quickly, looking away. He wondered if she felt it too. That same electric spark he felt in his fingertips when they touched.

He decided it wasn't something he needed to know. Hell no. He had to focus on Marjorie.

She was what mattered.

And hell, if he had an ally, a partner in Ellie, that was great.

But it was never going to be more.

CHAPTER 7

Over the next several days, Ellie and Clark settled into a routine with baby Marjorie.

In the morning, Ellie got up quite a bit later than Clark. He was up with the roosters, starting his workday on the ranch early. Since it was summer, Ellie enjoyed sleeping later. She had never been a morning person, and unfortunately the American school system—and indeed all of capitalism—demanded that a person acclimate to early mornings. So did small babies, apparently, though Marjorie woke later than cows and schoolchildren.

Ellie was usually up and around by seven thirty, after a night of somewhat broken sleep. Then she would make Marjorie her bottle and start on a fresh pot of coffee.

She had the whole house to herself during the day. And it was such a lovely home, so much nicer than the single room she'd had at Angelica's house. She really did appreciate the more luxurious surroundings, she had to admit.

She liked to believe she was past all that. After all, she knew that money didn't buy happiness.

But it did buy comfort. And this was more than comfortable.

At lunchtime, she made herself a sandwich and sat out on the back patio with Marjorie, enjoying the sunshine. She cleaned, because at the moment she didn't have work to occupy herself, so she didn't mind pitching in around the house.

Doing Clark's laundry was a little too intimate though. Touching his jeans, T-shirts, underwear. Anything that had been on that big, powerful body. It would start her thinking about his body, his muscles, and she would be a little bit of a mess.

She was a thirty-three-year-old woman; she wasn't a giddy teenager. She really needed to get over her sexual fixation.

He was her coparent.

That was all.

He was gorgeous, yes. But there were a lot of gorgeous men. Okay, there were not that many men as gorgeous as he was, who were also over six feet tall, incredibly capable, and good with children. But still. He was her partner in child-rearing. She didn't need him to be anything else. And even attempting to change their relationship would be a terrible risk.

Not that he had shown any interest.

Though there had been that moment the other day before dinner when their hands had touched. She'd felt a bolt of desire move through her body, and for a moment she'd been certain he felt it too. And then, just like that, she was sure she'd made it up. Which was a safer thing to assume anyway.

After lunch, she put Marjorie down for her nap and usually had a shower. And by the time she was finished, Clark was back and ready to start dinner. Even though he worked out on the ranch all day, dinner was his domain. She had to admit he was a better cook than she was.

She could prepare easy meals—spaghetti with jarred sauce, white people tacos, yeah, she pretty much had that down. But Clark knew what he was doing. He cooked beautiful steaks, roasted perfect chickens, and made legendary hamburgers, complete with homemade baked beans. That was what they were having tonight, along with generous handfuls of original potato chips. It was beyond a treat. And so was Clark's company, which she never would have imagined.

But that was before she had really gotten to know him. Before she'd realized he was the only other person in the world who was facing the same challenges she was, and that made him an ally, not an enemy.

They sat down at the dinner table together, with Marjorie nestled in the crook of his arm.

"So, how are the cows today?" she asked.

"Doing good," he said. "Why do you ask?"

"I realize that I don't ask what you do out there all day."

"Well. There are always fences to fix. There's always some disaster or another around the fence. Flood, or sometimes the dumb animals just run through the thing. Tree limbs, shifting ground, genuinely, it's always something. I'm constantly checking to make sure the cows don't decide to rehome themselves."

"Well, could you really blame them?"

"I guess not. After all, this is their fate," he said, gesturing to the hamburger on her plate.

She looked down at it, suddenly feeling slightly guilty.

"Oh no," he said. "You don't have a sense of humor about your food having feelings?"

"Not really," she said. Though she ended up taking another bite, because it was really good.

"Sometimes I'm moving the cows from one pasture to another, sometimes mowing the fields. There are all kinds of things to do."

"I'd love to see it."

"Sure. Why don't you come out tomorrow at lunchtime? I'll swing by and pick you up if you'll make us a picnic lunch."

"Okay," she said. "That sounds pretty fair."

"Well, I'm deeply concerned with fairness."

He grinned at her, and it made her heart race.

What was it about a big strong man and a tiny baby? The way

he held her, so gentle, when she knew he was strong enough to lift boulders. He was just so big, so solid, and yet the tenderness he exhibited with Marjorie was . . .

It made her breath catch. The way he held her now, eating dinner with one hand . . .

She needed to get it together.

She did not need to be indulging in lustful thoughts.

"All right. I'll make the sandwiches. And I'm sure Marjorie will love seeing the ranch too."

He looked down at the baby. "Everything the light touches is your kingdom," he said.

She laughed. "Oh, little Simba."

And at the same time, she felt overjoyed that he had this legacy for Marjorie.

That she was his to protect.

"My own dad is just so uninterested in us. I never felt that he wanted to show us anything. Protect us. Pass anything on to us. He's just so disconnected. It's easy to be angry at my mother. Really easy, because she's difficult. But I'm sure that having a husband who just didn't engage wasn't easy for her. And I don't know if she wanted more from him, if that dynamic suited them or . . . I don't know. What I do know is that it was never like this. Marjorie is so . . ." She realized that she was almost saying it: that Marjorie was lucky. But she didn't mean it in the way a couple of other people had said it. She didn't mean it in the sense that Clark was saintly to have agreed to take her on. She meant it in the sense that a dad like him was a singular, special thing.

How had she never realized, watching Clark take care of his brother over the years, show up endlessly, love unconditionally, that Clark was more than a good man?

He was exactly the kind of good man who would make a wonderful father, who was being a wonderful father, in action, right in front of her, even though he hadn't been prepared for it. She thought that men often got too much credit for doing the bare minimum, but that wasn't Clark.

Not at all.

And it was a funny thing, because when she had been rooming with Angelica, sometimes they had eaten dinner together, but sometimes not. Living here with Clark felt much more like being a family.

Not roommates. Not even simply coparents.

She felt a little sad, thinking ahead to a future when they wouldn't be sharing a home.

Wow. She had to stop that, because they weren't a nuclear family. They were just doing their very best to come together. It was tempting to give in to that fantasy, to take risks they had no business taking. She wanted to make a perfect picture out of something broken. But that could end disastrously.

If they actually tried to have a romantic relationship, and it went south, it would compromise Marjorie's future.

"Great," he said. "I'm looking forward to tomorrow's picnic."

He smiled at her. And she felt her heart flip.

Anxiety swirled in her stomach.

He wasn't the problem. She was. Her own feelings were. She needed to get hold of herself, so that she didn't blow everything up.

CHAPTER 8

The next day at lunchtime, he drove back to the ranch house and there were Marjorie and Ellie waiting for him. As pretty as a picture. And perfect.

He was doing his damn level best not to let his own feelings get in the way of their arrangement.

But it was hard. When they were sharing a house like this. Sharing a dinner table.

When the connection between Ellie and him was beginning to feel like something deeper than it actually was.

He was just so attracted to her. Sharing a small space with her, when they were in the kitchen for example, maneuvering around each other, was the world's most beautiful torture.

He didn't dislike it. But it was risky. Yeah. It was real damned risky.

When she smiled up at him as he took Marjorie from her arms and fastened her into the baby seat so they could head out onto the ranch, he had to stop himself from putting his hand against his chest to soothe the spot where his heart ached.

This was nothing like anything he'd ever experienced. He'd never seen a man and a woman working together to raise a child, to give that child the best they could offer.

No. His own parents had been so damn selfish.

This time with Ellie and Marjorie was giving him a glimpse at something he hadn't really believed existed. A glimmer of hope that he couldn't afford to obsess on.

As they drove away from the house, he tried to view the scenery through her eyes. He'd bought this piece of land two years earlier. Begun construction on the house a year and a half ago.

His dream. This place had always felt like a dream. The tall, stately mountains, the majestic pine trees.

The view of the valley below.

The ground here was volcanic. Red lava rock and black obsidian emerged from the ground in a great many places, and petrified wood was plentiful, including a grove of petrified trees that stood in his favorite spot on the property.

He paused his truck right in front of it. "This is a petrified forest," he said.

"On your property?" she asked, her eyes going wide.

The trees were thick, with jagged tops and bark that looked more like rock than wood. Veins of pale white and reddish brown ran down the length of them. The trunks stood in a circle, surrounded still by living pines that stretched up high toward the sky, the sun filtering down around them making them look like a pagan altar.

"Yeah," he said. "In the mid 1800s there was a series of eruptions in Oregon that lasted thirty years or so, and it formed a lot of the volcanic landscape here. But you're a teacher, so you probably know that."

"I don't teach science, so no, I don't. I don't know about volcanoes, but I could tell you about Zane Grey going to Rogue River."

"Then I can teach you about volcanoes and you can teach me about literature."

She laughed. "I'll let you in on a secret. I like literature just fine, but if I'm going to choose my own reading material, I prefer genre fiction. Give me thrillers, mysteries, and romance, thank you."

"I'm not a big reader. You'll have to recommend something to me. I'll have time to read now that I'm a homebody and a dad and not out riding in the rodeo."

The word made his heart catch in his chest. A dad. He was. And Ellie was a mother. Another thing they had in common was that they'd walked into that hospital as two single people and walked out as parents.

Silence settled between them, the only sound the pop of his engine as it cooled. "This is really beautiful," she whispered.

"Yeah. It gives me kind of a thrill, having a piece of this."

She looked sad, and he felt something shift inside him.

"It's really cool that you have this," she said.

He saw himself through her eyes then. A man who wanted to grab hold of something lasting because of everything he hadn't had way back then, and she wasn't really wrong.

He'd bought this place partly to flex his newfound success. Hell, it was part of why he'd come back to this town in the first place.

But now his motivation had shifted. Marjorie had shifted his purpose.

"She's going to love playing here," he said.

Suddenly, this place meant something else. It was different, and so was he. He didn't care if he was better than anyone else. He just cared that his little girl—yeah, his little girl—had the best place to play. "This is going to be like a magic portal," he said.

"A fairy forest," she agreed, immediately picking up his mood.

"She's going to be able to run all around here, bring her friends."

"And no one will get mad when they're noisy," she said.

"And it won't be embarrassing because it's a mess."

"And we won't make her vacuum when they're here. Or do her piano lessons or her ballet drills."

"And there will always be food in the pantry."

This was like making vows. The real creation of a family, then and there, in the presence of the petrified trees.

It was a deep, meaningful moment that he felt all the way down to his bones.

"Forever and ever," she said.

"Hell yeah," he said.

He put the truck back into drive, and they continued down to his main pasture, where most of the cattle were.

He drove the truck right through the field and parked it just a few feet away from the herd.

He took the car seat out of the truck as she got out the picnic basket, and he set Marjorie in her car seat in the truck bed. He and Ellie sat on the tailgate, situating the basket between them.

"Did you want with mustard or without?" she asked, holding a choice of two sandwiches out to him.

"With, thank you."

"I had a feeling. If you wanted without I was going to be in trouble. Because I don't like it."

He laughed. "Why didn't you just ask?"

She wrinkled her nose, and she was just so cute, it actually made him ache. "I don't know."

"You're a silly thing," he said.

The sun was warm, and the view was perfect.

The companionship was pretty good too.

"Your mom really made you practice the piano when you had friends over?" he asked.

"Yes," she said. "She was really strict. Like I said, there was no room for mistakes."

"And your sister's response to that was to jump into making all the biggest mistakes?"

"Yes."

"And your mom's not proud of you?"

"Not really. Because being a teacher doesn't make you a lot of money. However, people respect the profession. So, there's an element of it that she does like, in spite of herself."

"Well, when you actually do go talk to her about the baby, I want to go with you."

"I can't put it off anymore."

"Well, we had a good day today. Let's not make it bad. Tomorrow. We'll swing by tomorrow."

He was ready to handle any response the woman had to throw at them.

Ellie wasn't going to have to handle it alone.

Hell, as far as he was concerned, Ellie would never have to handle her mother alone again.

He would make sure of it.

Chapter 9

She'd called her mom and dad to let them both know that she'd be stopping by today, and now she was very nervously riding shotgun in Clark's truck on her way to the house she grew up in, a place that always made her feel as if she was about to swallow a cup of nails.

Maybe showing up with Clark was the wrong move.

But there was no right move here.

Clark had told her he wanted to tell his parents over the phone, because he needed to figure out what condition they were in, and it had been a few months since he'd seen them.

But she knew better than to give her mom serious news over the phone. That was the wrong move. Nancy had protocol for everything, and certain things should not be texted or delivered via phone.

The street looked the same as always, and the house just the way it had when she was growing up. She'd moved back to town at the beginning of the school year and had only been to dinner with her parents twice. She felt bad about it because she was the only child her parents had who would visit them, but it was just so complicated.

The truck pulled into the wide, paved driveway and she found herself staring at her mother's potted plants on the porch. Perfect and bright and cheery. So much time and maintenance and stress to look just so.

They got out of the truck, and she walked toward the front door, while Clark followed behind her with Marjorie in his arms.

She twisted her hands together and rocked back and forth on her heels. He put his hand on her arm, calming her nervous energy right then and there, his calloused palm on her elbow grounding her. Then warming her.

She looked up at him and felt reassured.

She knocked on the door.

A moment later, her mother opened it, and she felt her heart squeezing her chest. "Hi, Mom," she said. "I need to talk to you."

"What is this?" Her mom looked from Clark to her, and then at the baby.

"Melanie's," she said.

There was no perfect staging of conversations where her mother was concerned. There was no way to make this easy, no way to soften the blow or direct her response.

It was better to just get it out of the way. Better to just say what needed to be said.

"That's your sister's baby?" The expression on her mother's face couldn't be readily decoded.

"Yes."

"Come in."

She and Clark went into the house, which was as pristine as ever. A shining altar to her mother's anxiety.

"You can come to the living room," she said, leading them to the couch.

They sat down, and she looked over at Clark, who was

cradling Marjorie against his chest. She could feel the disapproval coming off her mother in waves. She wanted to shield Marjorie from it. And in a strange way, wanted to shield Melanie, too. Even though she wasn't here.

She wanted to shield Melanie from her mother's disdain. She wanted to protect everyone from what this moment's revelation was going to bring.

Even her mother, though Ellie could feel that the conversation was going to go very badly.

She didn't know how she knew that. Her mother was a master at hiding her true feelings. She was a master at smiling while inside she was seething.

"How old is she?"

"Just about a week."

"When did you find out?"

"The day she was born. We went to the hospital because Melanie and . . . Melanie and Ty both called."

"And what are you doing? Are you offering temporary placement? Why do you feel the need to tell me this happened?"

"Because we're keeping her," she said. "Clark and I. We're going to raise her."

"Oh, Ellie, you cannot keep letting your sister's mistakes derail your potential."

She sat there, stunned by her mother's words. "Derail my potential? What does that even mean?"

"You know what it means. You could've gone to a more prestigious school. You could've aimed higher if you weren't always dealing with Melanie's mistakes."

"How is this aiming too low, Mom? I'm taking care of my niece. I'm taking care of my family."

"What about *your* life? You're going to be stuck with a child that's . . ." Her mom looked at Clark. "A Porter. Part of that family. You're going to be stuck with them. Stuck with him."

"Mom," she said slowly. "I don't see it that way. That there's something wrong with the Porter family. Melanie has the exact same problems as some of the Porters. She and Ty chose their path. But they also chose to do the best, most compassionate thing for their child. They chose to do what needed to be done."

"And we're choosing to give Marjorie the best life possible," Clark said. "I don't need you to like me. You can treat me with all the disdain you like, but you will not treat this little girl with even an ounce of it."

This was the first time her mom had heard the name. Had heard whom they'd named her after, and she didn't even react.

"Mr. Porter . . ."

"I'm not here to be scolded. Ellie wants to maintain a relationship with you, and it matters to her. It doesn't matter to me, though, so I would be careful about what I said if I were you. Because I might tell you some things about yourself that you won't be able to forget."

He stood up, and Ellie stood up with him. "It's up to you, Mom," Ellie said. "How involved we'll be in each other's lives. My first responsibility is to Marjorie."

"You always chose your sister," her mother said. "You chose her over me. Over our relationship. Look at what she's done to you. To me. Everyone in town whispers about her. She's the black sheep. She's always manipulating you. Making you feel sorry for her. She's made her choices. And she doesn't need you to enable her."

"I'm not enabling her. I love her. And maybe she needed me because she knew she didn't have you. Knew she didn't have Dad. But in any case, I've made my choices for my life. I love my job. I didn't need to go to a better school. I didn't need to live somewhere else. I don't need to live my life to make you proud of your own. Marjorie certainly will never have to do that for me."

Clark led the way out of the room, and she followed as quickly as possible. It wasn't until she was out the door that she realized she was shaking.

"Are you okay?" he asked.

"Of all the things, I didn't expect her to tell me that I was going to ruin my life by taking care of Marjorie. I guess I didn't expect that she would want to get rid of her own granddaughter."

"Well, she's half Porter."

She looked at him, her heart twisting. "I'm sorry she said that."

"I don't need an apology. It's how a lot of people feel."

"But it's not fair. I meant what I said. You're like me, Clark. You hold the line for the person in your family who's most vulnerable. And we both do it because we know that's what love is."

He nodded. "Yeah. It is."

"Just because you're used to being treated badly by people in town, that doesn't mean you have to accept it."

"I don't accept it," he said. "I've never accepted it. Why do you think I went off to the rodeo? Why do you think I bought this ranch? Because I've always thought I was better than these people let me be. Because I've always thought I could do something with my life. I'm not mad about it, though. I don't need to fight against it. Every day, I fight against anything that could send me down a path I don't want to be on. I don't have time to fight other people. Especially not when a lot of what they say is true. The best revenge is living well. I just live well. Not angry. Not tangled up with people who wouldn't like me no matter how much I succeed. Who wouldn't like me no matter what."

"Well. I'm mad for you. And I'm mad for Marjorie. Because she deserves better than a grandmother who looks at an innocent baby and thinks such negative things. And better than a grandfather who will barely look at her at all."

"You're not going to get much better with my side of the family. My parents can be good. When they're actually present. But that's not often."

"I'm just . . . I don't understand why family has to be so hard."

"It's a good question. I hear that some people really enjoy spending time with their family."

"I want that for her," she said.

He looked at her, and her heart turned over in her chest. "So do I."

Chapter 10

Her mom started texting apologies almost immediately after they left, but it took a couple of weeks for Ellie to respond.

Even longer to agree to meet her mom for lunch.

But she told Nancy in no uncertain terms that she and Clark were adopting Marjorie together, and that if she wanted to be in her granddaughter's life, she wouldn't be speaking to anyone the way she had that day they'd come to visit.

Ellie and Clark got their court date surprisingly quickly. And because they were the baby's aunt and uncle, because the parental rights had been signed away with no coercion or second thoughts, the adoption went smoothly.

After two months of living with Clark and Ellie, Marjorie was ready to be adopted.

Ellie dressed the baby in an outfit that was essentially a giant ruffle, and put on a pink sundress of her own. Clark was wearing black jeans, black cowboy boots, a black T-shirt, and a black hat. And he looked mouthwatering.

Honestly, it was getting harder and harder to be in close proximity with this man all the time and not have inappropriate thoughts about him.

She would have thought that it would get easier. That she would get used to him, or something.

But no.

If anything, it got more difficult the longer she was exposed to his pheromones, or whatever the attraction was.

It was so strange, because on many days she felt more grown-up than she ever had.

The house was a very real house. Very adult.

And Clark was a real adult roommate. Unlike Jason, who'd propped things up on cardboard boxes and played video games for half the night.

Clark just had it all together.

But in many ways, she felt more like a teenager than she ever had. Obsessing over a brush of his hand against hers when he passed the salt at dinner. Thinking about him before she went to sleep.

Getting giddy when he came in at dinnertime.

Yeah. She was more than a little bit of a lost cause.

Today, she needed to channel the most mature version of herself, not the one that was losing it over a cute boy.

She had to coparent with him.

Then she got emotional. Her eyes filled with tears as the truck pulled up to the courthouse.

"Are you okay?"

"We're really doing this. She's going to be ours."

It was a strange thing, because they would share a baby, but they would be separate. Distinctly so.

And that made this moment feel just a little bit . . . less unified, maybe, than it should. It shouldn't make a difference. And yet she found that it did.

She sat there while he lifted Marjorie out of her car seat, and then she got out of the passenger seat and stepped onto the lawn of the courthouse.

He carried their daughter—Marjorie was really going to be officially and legally their daughter at the end of this hearing—and she followed along with him.

And then just as they got to the bottom of the steps, with Marjorie still curled into his right arm, he reached out and took her hand. The touch of his skin against hers was electric. His palm was calloused from all that hard labor. His hands much rougher than she'd imagined.

Her heart began to pound harder, and she wasn't sure if it was because they were headed into the courtroom or if it was just because of his touch.

She looked at him, and the heat in his eyes did something to her.

Oh, Clark.

They walked inside the building and up to the reception area, which was enclosed in glass. The woman behind the glass hit a button so that she could speak to them through a microphone.

"Name?"

"Porter and Parks. We have an appointment in Family Court." His voice was so sure and strong. Everything about him was sure and strong.

They got their passes, and were buzzed back into the courtrooms, where they waited until their number was called.

When they walked into the room, they were joined by Daisy, the attorney representing Marjorie, and of course, the judge.

They went through the process, each of them answering questions and passing the signed petition to the judge, who granted it instantly.

"I'd like to make a special acknowledgment of the biological parents. Their signing over their rights rather than putting their daughter through the system for years, years of struggling with their addictions, was a selfless and caring gesture on their part. Reunification is always a good goal, but it's also an outcome that happens far less often than any of us would like. And in this case, I'm grateful that not only did the biological parents have placement they thought would be ideal for their child, but they made it easy."

Ellie was grateful for that too.

When they were finished, the judge descended from his bench and held Marjorie for a moment.

Emotions swelled in Ellie's chest. It felt like a coming together. Their being able to care for Marjorie. Her having a place to be.

So much love had gone into every step of this adoption. Starting with Melanie and Ty. Even if some people couldn't understand that.

The judge had. That mattered.

It really mattered.

Because when she told Marjorie about all of this, she would mention that fact.

That even in court, the role her biological parents had played in her future was appreciated, acknowledged. And that it mattered.

They'd gone into the courtroom as three separate people holding on to each other and walked out as a family. Whatever she and Clark were to each other, they would always be Marjorie's parents.

And that was an amazing, humbling thing to realize.

An incredible and awe-inspiring gift.

"Should we go out to dinner?" Clark asked.

Yes. It would be their very first meal as a family.

"Let's go to the Italian restaurant back in Caldwell."

"All right. Fancy."

She laughed. "It's a fancy day."

"I suppose it is."

It was more than a fancy day. It was the beginning of something. It was the beginning of their family.

And for the first time in more years than she could remember, Ellie felt more whole than she did broken.

Chapter 11

The adoption had been one of the most profound experiences of Clark's life. He'd felt like Marjorie's father ever since she had been put in his arms. But it was official now. Recognized by the state.

And the responsibility, beautiful and heavy, had been sitting on his shoulders since that night in the hospital.

He felt no regret. It was what he wanted. He knew it down to his bones.

Marjorie was a pretty good sleeper, but there were times when she resisted falling asleep.

And there were times when getting sleep was damned near impossible.

The sound of her crying filtered over the baby monitor, and Clark turned over in bed, sighing heavily. It was his night on duty. He was exhausted. But he also didn't think that Ellie should take on more than her fair share of sleepless nights. She might not be working full time at the moment, but they both had flexible schedules, and he intended to do his part.

He got out of bed and walked quietly toward the nursery,

moving easily through the hallway illuminated by moonlight shining through the skylights above.

He walked into the cheerful pink room, and picked Marjorie up, cradling her to his chest. "All right. Settle down, sweetheart," he said. "Do you need to eat?"

He carried the baby down to the kitchen, and started to make a bottle.

He hummed softly to himself. God, he couldn't remember humming absently ever in his life. That was the habit of a different sort of person. Someone who had joy in his heart. Hope for the future.

He looked down at Marjorie. She felt like hope. Like the hope of something really good. Something he'd believed for a long time he couldn't have.

And he thought of the beautiful woman sleeping down the hall from him.

His gut went tight, his heart starting to beat faster.

Yeah. It was really tempting to fantasize that their relationship could be something more than it was.

Really tempting to create a whole narrative around that.

But that was one hope too far. A wish too many.

He'd never been one to wish too intently on anything.

But becoming Marjorie's father was a miracle. Maybe that meant there could be more.

Or maybe it meant he'd had plenty. Wasn't ever going to have another in his lifetime.

After all, he'd already improved his circumstances financially. Wasn't it a little bit greedy to want it all?

"Oh, I thought I heard something."

He looked up and saw Ellie standing in the doorway, wearing a large T-shirt that just covered the tops of her thighs.

God Almighty.

"Hey. You don't need to wake up," he said. "My job right now."

He needed to keep his distance from her. Because even in the dim lighting, she was far too beautiful for his own good. Even now, he was torturing himself with quick, full-color fantasies that he had no business having about her.

"It's fine," she said. "I wasn't sleeping very well anyway."

"Any particular reason?"

"This whole situation?" She sighed. "I want to do the best I can for Marjorie. I want to be better than my family, that's for sure. My parents weren't the family I wanted."

He laughed. "I don't blame you. I'd like to send mine back too."

"But we have Marjorie. And we have each other."

That squeezing sensation in his chest grew more intense. "Yeah. I'm grateful for that."

He finished feeding Marjorie the bottle, and Ellie walked toward him. His heart went tight. She reached out and took the baby, cradling her gently to her breast. Then she looked up at him, and his eyes dropped down to her mouth. They had a baby between them right now. They always did. He was beginning to wonder if they were purposely avoiding moments like this. Avoiding the change that might come. How one touch could transform something innocent into something a whole lot more.

"I can take her back upstairs. She'll need a diaper change."

"Yeah," he said. "Sure."

She turned away from him and started up the stairs. He held on to the counter, trying to calm the raging heat inside his body.

This was over the top. There was too much going on. He couldn't afford to be reacting to her this way.

Was it unresolved childhood longing? A deep need to finally have the love he'd wanted back when he hadn't felt worthy?

But that wasn't a good reason to kiss her.

Lord Almighty.

He was a grown-ass man with tons of experience. Getting wound up about a kiss seemed stupid.

Getting bothered about a theoretical kiss, one that existed only in his mind, that seemed even more stupid.

But here he was. Obsessing about what it would be like for his mouth to touch Ellie's.

He was going to have to go out and find sexual partners so he didn't spend all his time obsessing about her.

The very idea made him feel uneasy.

He didn't want somebody else.

He wanted her. If he were honest with himself, he'd wanted her for a very long time.

His body had reached its limit, apparently.

He got a grip on himself as best he could and then headed up the stairs. Right as she was coming out of the nursery.

And then it was just the two of them, standing in the hall, in the moonlit darkness. He could hear her breathing, his own heart beating so hard in his chest, he thought it might explode.

"She's down," she said.

"Good. We should both get some sleep."

"Yes," she agreed.

She looked at her hands, just for a moment, and he fought the urge to reach out and grip her chin between his thumb and forefinger. To ask her to look at him. He fought the urge that had existed inside him since he was sixteen years old. All the urges he hadn't been able to follow, and suddenly he was really angry at his younger brother.

Because Ty had taken one of the Parks sisters and smashed her up.

And in doing so he had prevented Clark from ever being able to touch the woman he'd wanted for half his life.

It didn't seem fair. He'd spent all these years suppressing that anger.

He'd spent all these years trying so hard to be on Ty's side. To just be his older brother. To love him in the way he ought to.

And it had kept him from this.

He wanted to touch her.

She looked up at him, her eyes meeting his, and he heard her breath catch.

"You're so pretty," he whispered.

She froze then, mid-breath, her lips parted just slightly. And he felt an ache bloom in his stomach. Spread outward. He felt his entire body heat.

His heart beating fast and hard, he followed his impulse and lifted his hand, touched her chin.

She closed her eyes, her breath coming out in a shaky gust.

"You've always been so beautiful," he whispered.

She opened her eyes, and it was as if reality slammed hard against his chest.

He dropped his hand, took a step away. "I'm glad I have you," he said quickly. "Glad she has you."

A reminder of why they were here. Why they were standing in this darkened hallway? It had nothing to do with them. With their attraction to each other.

He turned away from her and went back down the hallway toward his room. He closed the door behind him, and he locked it. Because he didn't trust himself. He didn't trust himself not to take what he wanted.

And the hardest part was that he could see she wanted him too. He didn't know for how long. He didn't know if it was a recent attraction or something that had been burning inside her for years, but he knew it was there. And that meant he needed to stay far, far away. That meant he couldn't let his guard down.

No. He had to be vigilant. He had to protect this new family of theirs. And that meant not trying and failing at having a relationship with her.

He had been strong for a long damned time. He just had to go on being strong.

Chapter 12

Picnicking with Ellie and Marjorie was becoming a semi-regular event. Today, they'd opted to take their lunch to the petrified forest. Marjorie was lying on her blanket, kicking her feet in the sun, and he and Ellie were sitting on their blanket, eating their sandwiches.

"It's the strangest thing, Ellie," he said. "We've seen each other in crisis mode all the time. And now we're seeing each other in parenting mode. What did you do in the years between all of that?"

"I went to school," she said. "Had a couple of failed relationships."

"You mentioned the man baby."

She laughed. "Yes. There was the man baby. I had a boyfriend in college who was far more interested in binge drinking than studying, which was weird because when I met him, he seemed like kind of a nerd. But eventually he figured out that if he drank enough, people were happy to have him at parties. And that was the direction he went. And that's pretty much it."

"What about teaching?"

"Oh, I started at a private school. It was interesting, but not for me, ultimately."

"Why not?"

"Oh, nothing specific. It was fine. I was part of the living rosary."

"You . . . you're not Catholic."

"No. But the school was. It's a fun one to use in Two Truths and a Lie."

"I bet."

"The thing I love the most is connecting with kids. Getting them excited about reading. So the best teaching positions I've had were at schools that were willing to let me choose books that would get the kids interested in reading. That often meant graphic novels and books by younger, diverse authors with different worldviews. Kids get tired of reading the same dusty books. I love the classics, but I believe you have to mix them in with more contemporary literature so that kids understand that there are books for everyone. And that books can be written by people who look like them. People who think like them. And even more importantly, people who don't think like them. Because everyone has the freedom to write and express their views on things. And if you read something, and you really don't like it, you can write your own book. Add your ideas to the conversation. We always need more information, not less."

"You're a radical," he said.

"I'm a literature teacher. I should be a radical. By definition."

"All right. I like that."

"What about you? What have you been doing during all the in-between?"

"Winning championships, mostly. There was one year when I had a pretty gnarly injury. I think we saw each other. It was the night we were down at that honky-tonk in Albany. When I was trying to get Ty out, he threw a punch at me and hit me, because I was extra slow since I had broken ribs."

"Oh. I didn't know that."

"I didn't want to advertise it. But anyway. Yeah. I won a lot, invested a lot, because in careers like mine, you have to. Your body doesn't want to get thrown around like that forever. Being in rodeo is like being any professional athlete. You know you're not doing it forever, and you have to figure out where your money is going to come from in the future. So I did that."

"You mentioned before that you had endorsements."

"Yeah. Western apparel–focused, so probably not something you saw."

"Wait. Are you telling me you were modeling?"

He narrowed his eyes. "They were endorsement deals. Sponsorships."

"But you posed in ads for them."

"Yes," he said.

"I guess that's where being dangerously handsome gets really useful."

He laughed. "Well. Only if you're winning."

Right then, he had the urge to ask if she really thought he was handsome. It mattered.

He wished that it didn't.

"Why rodeo, though?"

"Because when you do that, you're connected to your body. You get a rush, but you don't need any substances. I'm not an adrenaline junkie. What I like about it is the clarity. The full experience of being present in your body in that moment. It's not like anything else. And it reminds me of who I am every time."

"Were you ever worried about what your life was going to look like when you didn't have that anymore?"

"A little. That's why I made plans to run this ranch. It's why I had the house built, I suppose."

"You suppose?"

"It's just such a big house for one person."

"Well, now you have two extra people."

He looked at her, his heart going tight, certainty taking hold of him.

Yeah. There were two other people. Living with her for the last couple months had been good. It had given him an immense feeling of peace. And having her there with Marjorie was . . . That was family. They were family.

He wanted her.

Yes, it was risky. Because if they tried, and they didn't succeed, where would that leave this little family?

One thing he knew about her, the same thing he knew about himself, was that they fought to do the right thing.

They had done it over and over again where their siblings were concerned. They would do it for Marjorie too.

So maybe they didn't need to hold back. Maybe he didn't need to.

Maybe he could have this.

Her. In the way he'd always wanted.

The very idea made his blood run hotter. Faster.

Yeah. He loved this domestic life. But he wanted something more. He wanted to explore the passion he felt with her. The heat he felt simmering between them every time there was a quiet moment. Like this one.

He wanted to touch her. But somehow, he knew this wasn't quite the right moment.

He could wait. Hell. He'd been waiting all this time. But one thing was sure. He wanted her.

And he was going to claim her.

Make her his wife.

God.

He loved her.

That realization was like an arrow being driven straight through his chest.

He loved her.

This wasn't a crush. It wasn't simple lust.

It had been her from the beginning. Every time he'd seen her. Even when she was angry at him.

It was her strength, her integrity, that drew him. Everything she was.

Her beauty called to his body. Everything she was called to his soul.

He had loved her all this time.

And now he just needed to wait for the right moment. The moment when she would be able to return his love.

CHAPTER 13

Generally speaking, she was doing okay with her attraction to Clark. She did a decent job not remembering that moment in the hallway when he'd touched her cheek. She had dinner with him, picnics, she talked to him about the future—though somehow they never discussed when she was going to move out—and she managed not to imagine what it would be like to kiss him.

Well, she didn't let herself imagine it every day.

She shivered. Then she wrapped her robe more tightly around herself and went down the stairs.

It was six thirty, early for Ellie, though Clark would already be out and working on the ranch.

But when she entered the kitchen, there he was, dressed for the day's work, looking gorgeous. She could have turned around, hightailed it right back up the stairs, and waited for him to leave. Not let him know she was there.

Well. At least this time she was wearing pants.

"Good morning."

"Morning," he said, sounding sleepy.

"You're getting kind of a late start."

"I didn't sleep that well last night."

She wanted to ask him why. She also knew better than to do that. Because she knew why. It was the same thing that was dogging her. She wouldn't say that she was the sort of person who was driven by physical attraction, but her physical attraction to him was like nothing she'd ever experienced before. Well. Except with him.

She took a step toward him and pointed toward the coffee maker. "I just want to get . . . I could just use some . . ."

"Yeah," he said.

He abruptly put his coffee mug down on the counter and walked toward her. He wrapped his arm around her, and pulled her up against his body, and she gasped.

She should tell him it was a bad idea. She should tell him not to.

She didn't. Instead she looked up at him, her heart threatening to pound its way out of her chest. She didn't move. And when he lowered his head and claimed her mouth with his, she reached up and clung to his shoulders, doing everything she could to keep herself from melting into the floor.

She'd never been kissed like this. He was masterful. Passionate. Even in the early morning, the whiskers on his face were rough. His mouth hot. His tongue slick. His body was just so big and hard and wonderful. She wanted to cling to him forever.

She'd never kissed a man who was so tall. He gathered her up in his arms, holding her on her tiptoes as he kissed her.

She felt as if her entire body was suffused with warmth. Need poured through her like honey.

She returned the kiss with enthusiasm, answering each slide of his tongue against hers.

"Clark," she whispered.

How did she tell him? How did she tell him that she had wanted this for so long? That one of the reasons she was so wound up every time he was near her was that there was always this need, throbbing beneath the surface. This thing she had no control over.

This thing that made her feel shame.

Though not for the reasons it once had. She felt shame now because the reason he had felt like such an illicit craving was tied up in what she believed about his family.

Shame that she hadn't realized immediately what a good man he was.

Such a good man.

He pulled away from her. "I've wanted to do that for years."

The raw admission almost stunned her into total silence. But she managed to squeak a question through her tightened throat. "Really?"

"Yes," he said. "You know you were the most beautiful girl I'd ever seen?"

Of course. Back when they were young. Before he got on the rodeo circuit. Before he'd been exposed to thousands of beautiful women.

"What are you doing?"

"What?" she asked, sounding dazed.

"You're looking at me like you don't believe me. Or like you're trying to find some reason to pull apart what I said. Don't pull it apart. Just take the compliment."

"I was just . . . never mind."

"You're still the most beautiful woman I've ever seen."

She felt as if her heart were being torn in two. "Clark. We have to raise a baby together."

"Yeah. I know," he said, taking a step away from her. "But I'm glad I got to kiss you. You know, I always imagined it would happen at night. Our first kiss."

"You thought about our first kiss?"

"Hell yeah," he said. "I figured it would happen at night. Maybe during a thunderstorm. There would be lightning, and the earth would shake. But yeah. You're right. We're raising a baby together. And that's the most important thing. But I'm glad I got to do it."

She took a step away, her throat feeling tight. She was good at this. Self-denial. She was good at doing what needed to be done, and stepping away was something that needed to be done.

She and Clark didn't know the first thing about relationships. Not real, long-term ones. Not the kind that made families.

It was so tempting.

Her urge to take a kiss and turn it into a whole lifetime was exhibit A about why they couldn't make it as a couple. The stakes would always feel too high. The risk would always be too great, and the probability of failure would always be too likely.

"I gotta go to work."

"I need to drink my coffee."

"I'll see you later."

She brooded for the rest of the day, and in the late afternoon she stood on the back patio, watching as gray clouds rolled in.

I thought maybe it would be during a thunderstorm.

She tried not to dwell on his words.

She wondered about the psychological reason behind that kiss. Was it just that they were a man and a woman living in a house together, attracted to each other, and looking for a connection that felt so familiar? That felt like it was the recognizable shape of a family?

Was it just hormones?

Or was it something deeper?

Something that had been stirring inside her for longer than she was letting herself admit.

Thunder rolled, and it echoed through her. She thought about what he'd said.

About the lightning striking. That's what his kiss had been like.

He'd always felt off-limits. She'd told herself that was why she'd been so attracted to him.

Why sometimes when they went to deal with their siblings, she'd imagined immediately booking their own room in that rent-by-the-hour motel and burning off the heat between them.

That was why her brain hounded her with intrusive thoughts about him.

Because those thoughts were taboo.

Now she'd let herself kiss him, though, and her longing was more than just the lure of the forbidden. It was chemistry such as she'd never experienced before.

She sighed heavily, turned, and went back into the house. Marjorie was cooing in her little baby swing, looking up at the dangling cherries and bananas on the mobile above her head. The little swing was set up right in the living area, and Marjorie was beginning to enjoy watching everything.

Marjorie was, at least, a good distraction.

She could give thanks for the occasional exhaustion she felt after staying up with the baby all night, because it stopped her from obsessing about Clark. When she wasn't thinking about Marjorie, she fantasized like a teenage girl. All over again.

Except now she was old enough to do something about her fantasies.

She made herself a sandwich and hid up in her room instead of joining Clark for dinner, which felt cowardly. Particularly since she kept Marjorie with her, giving her a bottle in bed while she ate the sandwich with her other hand. He could've come looking for her. He didn't.

Maybe he needed a reprieve as badly as she did.

When she finished she crept silently out of the room and into the nursery. She read Marjorie a book, gave her a bath in her bathroom, and rocked her for a long while before putting her in the crib.

It was very unusual for Clark to stay away, and she felt guilty that he was doing it now.

But as she exited the space she realized that the baby monitor was still in Clark's room.

She would have to sneak in and grab it. She hadn't heard him come up the stairs, so she was reasonably sure he was not there yet. His bedroom door was cracked open, and she walked in just as the bathroom door opened and Clark stepped out, his lower half barely covered by a towel.

"Oh," she said, standing there staring at him like a deer caught in the headlights.

He had just gotten out of the shower. His hair was wet, his skin glistening. His muscles were the epitome of masculine glory, his chest the sort of sculpted wonder that poets could compose sonnets about. Or at least, she could, and she didn't particularly like poetry. A shameful thing for an English teacher to admit, but it just didn't move her.

However, the stanzas created inside her body by the ripple of his ab muscles were really making her rethink.

"What are you doing in here?"

"The baby monitor," she said, gesturing to it on the nightstand.

"Oh, Ellie, we are really in trouble now."

The thunder rolled outside. Like a commandment.

Without thinking about it, she closed the door, slowly and softly until it clicked.

"Are you sure you want this?" he asked.

"Yes," she whispered.

He walked toward her, dropping the towel and exposing the rest of his body to her hungry gaze.

She was about to say something. Something she shouldn't say, something very inappropriate—and she wasn't the kind of person who made comments like that to a lover—when he claimed her mouth. Didn't wait. Didn't pause. Didn't hesitate.

It was a bad idea for all the reasons they'd already discussed.

It was bad. But it was oh so good. It was something she couldn't turn away from. It was something she didn't even want to deny.

She wanted him. With everything she had in her.

She wanted him, because he was wonderful. Because he was

perfect. The most beautiful man, the most glorious man, the best caregiver for Marjorie, the most loving brother to Ty, even when Ty was difficult. And by extension, he'd also been there for Melanie.

Most of all, he'd been there for her.

She hadn't thought of it that way at the time, but Clark was someone she could count on. Clark was always there. Always there when they were bailing out their siblings. Always there when things were as hard as they ever got.

And right now, he was hard against her. Right now, he was everything.

She threw her entire self into the kiss, arching her back against him, letting her breasts rub against that hard chest. She wanted to be naked.

"I haven't had sex for like, three years," she said.

He held the back of her head, staring intently into her eyes. "Oh," he said.

"Has it been three years for you?"

He shook his head.

But then he cupped her face, thumb sliding over her cheekbones. "It hasn't been three years. But it's never been you."

That was all she needed to hear. It was all she ever needed to hear.

He stripped her shirt off, took her bra off with one clever flex of his fingers.

Then she was finally skin to skin with him as he continued to kiss her, his hands moving over her back. Going to the snap of her jeans, taking the zipper down slowly.

She was naked, held up against his body, and it was surreal.

Beautiful. The fulfilment of a dream she'd never really let herself have.

Desire was driving her, but there was something more, something deeper. Something she'd never shared with another man, not ever.

He lifted his hands, cupped her breasts, squeezed hard, drawing his thumbs over her nipples, and a shuddering gasp escaped her mouth.

"You really want me," he said, his voice filled with wonder.

"Yes. I wanted you in high school. I wanted you even when I didn't fully know what it meant. I fantasized about you even when I didn't know exactly what I was fantasizing about."

"And you were so goddamn mean to me," he said, his voice a low growl as he dragged his thumb over her nipple again. One more time. And again.

She shuddered. "I know. I had to be. Otherwise I was going to break. I couldn't afford to break. We can't afford to break now."

"I'm fucking shattered, babe," he said, closing the distance between them and claiming her mouth in the most intense kiss of her life. She ached between her legs, her flesh slick, her entire body so close to the edge a slight breeze could send her toppling over.

He backed her up against the wall, hand going between her thighs as he began to trace a pattern of torture over her sensitized flesh.

She arched against him, gave herself over to him, clung to his shoulders as he pushed her closer and closer to the peak.

The cry that escaped her lips shocked her, but not as much as how quickly, how easily he took her to the summit.

And even before she came back down, he built it up again. Swallowing the cry of pleasure on her lips before lifting her up and carrying her over to the bed.

He deposited her in the center of it, kissing her lips, her neck, a fiery trail down her body. He sucked her nipple deep into his mouth, and she arched up off the mattress, calling his name over and over again.

It was more than she had ever imagined it could be. *They* were more.

She had let herself believe that they were nothing but a mess. Nothing but fight or flight. Nothing but casualties in the devastation of their siblings' lives. But they were their own thing. Right now. This was them. It had nothing to do with anyone else.

Marjorie had brought them together.

But this was about them.

The years of not being able to explore their feelings. The years of denying what they felt. This was about the two of them.

And all the years that had been taken from them.

Because who knew what would've happened if the first Parks to kiss a Porter had been Ellie and Clark. Who knew what would've happened if they were the ones who had embarked on a teenage love affair.

Would she have supported Clark through his rodeo ambition?

Would he have lived in the city so that she could get her teaching career established? Would they be married with a family?

She was getting ahead of herself. Advancing their relationship much further than it ought to be, she knew. But the touch of his hands was like the promise of forever, and she couldn't shut off the scroll of emotion unfurling inside her.

He kissed her, and she was drowning. Her heart beating hard.

As the rain poured down outside, and the thunder rolled, she knew she was right where she needed to be.

He slid his hands down her waist, gripped her hips. Her stomach went tight.

She wasn't afraid.

He moved away from her, went and opened up a cabinet in the bathroom.

He returned a few moments later with a box of condoms, taking the time to protect them both before he returned to the bed.

Then as he kissed her, he thrust deep inside her. The closeness, the intensity of it took her breath away.

It was perfect. And so was he.

As he began to move, she clung to his shoulders, the wave of desire between them building and building.

And then when it hit, she cried out his name, clinging to his shoulders and arching against him, her release going on and on.

She'd had sex before. But it was never this.

Never brought this soul-crushing intensity. Never this beautiful, bright and shining triumph.

It was never something that made her feel complete. But he did.

He really, really did.

"Oh, Ellie," he said.

"I know," she replied.

"We should've done that a long time ago."

"I know," she said. "I wanted to. Honestly. I knew back in high school. But I thought it was like . . . you know, the teenage urge to rebel. And then when Melanie actually did it, I . . . I was sure it was wrong. I was sure there was something inside me that was primed for rebellion. Against all that ruthless perfection in our house. But I didn't want to end up like her."

"Everything that has been between us got caught up in Melanie and Ty. There was no way to get around that," he said. "Not for a long time."

"It was just really difficult."

"Yes," he agreed. "It was. Ellie, I've wanted you for years. I've loved you for years."

"What?"

"I do. I love you. I want to make a family with you. I understand that all of this is crazy. We have a baby to care for. And all of this baggage. Maybe I'm trying to make something perfect out of something imperfect, but I don't think so. Because it's always been you. I asked myself repeatedly who I was building this house for. I didn't have an answer. And yet, here it is, ready for a family. Ready for something that I didn't even have the faintest glimmer of. Then there was Marjorie. And you walked into the hospital. I knew you'd be there. Because in these situations you always were. All those times we met up. In the worst places. The worst bars, the seediest motels. It was all leading up to that meeting. And that's the one that brought us here."

He touched her face. "I needed to make a success of myself. I thought I wanted to show the town. I thought, sometimes, I wanted to show you. It wasn't about showing you, though. It was about becoming the right man for you. It was about becoming good enough to be your husband."

Her heart fluttered. "My husband?"

"Yes. God, it's always been you. It's never going to be anybody else. I realize that I'm moving quickly. You don't have to say yes to me right now. I realize the idea of getting married is a little bit out there, but we can wait. I just need you to know that's where I see it going. That's where I want it to go."

What more did she want?

She'd dated men who hadn't really understood her. Clark understood her. He knew her family. He knew everything she'd been through. He understood what it meant to love a sibling who was lost to the throes of addiction. To try to put boundaries on that person, but never to abandon them.

He was there for Marjorie. He knew she was a priority. He'd faced her mother down and hadn't flinched.

He had gone and made something of himself. Something amazing.

And she loved him.

That was the bottom line.

It was so clear. So wonderfully, perfectly clear.

And he was worthy of love. The love of a wife, the love of a brother, the love of a daughter.

The way he took care of Marjorie was one of the most beautiful things she'd ever seen.

The way he loved that little girl . . .

Yes. He was the man she wanted to be the father of her children. He was the one she wanted more than anything.

This wasn't rushing into things. This was fifteen years in the making.

Their love had undergone a trial by fire. It had already stood the test of time.

And it was glorious.

"I love you too. I put up so many barriers, trying to keep you at arm's length. I felt like it was too complicated. I felt like I couldn't trust myself. But that was all just fear. Fear of such strong feelings inside me. Fear of wanting something more than I wanted to be there for Melanie. But by giving us Marjorie, my sister gave us something to live for, something bigger than her and Ty's problems."

"I believe we can make a bright and beautiful future for our girl. For us."

"Yes," she said. She kissed him, her heart swelling with joy. "The next time we go to a courthouse, it will be for our wedding."

"Oh hell no, girl. We're not having a courthouse wedding. You're going to get everything."

A real wedding? But that meant involving her family, and that made her nervous.

But then suddenly the nerves dissipated.

She and Clark and Marjorie were their own family.

They were a family, and that mattered more than anything else.

She and Clark had love. They had Marjorie.

They had hope.

Epilogue

They raised Marjorie to know the whole story about her parents. Ellie and Clark never hid the way she came to be with them.

Because it was nothing to be ashamed of. Her birth parents' decision to give her up had been selfless. It had been an act of great strength, and it had come at a time when they hadn't had much strength available to them. Now, at sixteen, she was well-adjusted, and an amazing older sister to her four younger siblings.

Ellie and Clark's wedding took place when Marjorie was a year old, and it almost ended Ellie's relationship with her parents. It didn't, though. She had a complete meltdown with her mother and her father in the weeks leading up to it, but rather than breaking the ties between them, somehow, it had actually effected change.

Over the years, Ellie's mom had been able to create a good relationship with her grandchildren. She was easier with them than with her own children.

She let them finger paint at the kitchen table.

She let them make messes.

It was around the time of Marjorie's kindergarten graduation, when Ellie had been pregnant with their second biological child, that her mother finally made peace with Clark.

Seeing him with Marjorie had suddenly broken something inside her. Made her see who he truly was. That he was good. Better than her own husband, who was more interested in his grandchildren than he'd ever been in his children.

The change in her father made Ellie feel a bit resentful sometimes, because she knew it had to do with the fact that she and Clark had four sons, and her dad seemed far more comfortable with little boys than he had ever been with little girls.

But it was something she chose to let go. Because family was too important. In all its messy, difficult glory.

If her parents had been unkind to the kids, ever, if they had made them feel they were a problem, then Ellie wouldn't have hesitated to cut them off. But that wasn't how things had gone, she was grateful for that.

When Marjorie was thirteen, Melanie started writing her letters.

Ellie and Clark always screened them, but they shared them with her, and eventually, stopped looking at them beforehand, as Marjorie began to develop her own relationship with Melanie.

When Melanie and Ty reached eighteen months of sobriety, just at Marjorie's sixteenth birthday, Ellie and Clark decided it was time for them to meet their daughter.

Marjorie was dressed up, and they had a reservation at the best Italian restaurant in town—the same one they'd gone to the day Marjorie's adoption had been finalized. Today, they needed a whole private room for the celebration, because Melanie, Ty, and the four younger kids, Clark, Ellie, and Marjorie were all going to be there.

"How are you feeling?" Ellie asked Marjorie before they walked in. She rubbed her daughter's back, just as she'd done when she was a little girl.

"I'm good," she said. "Melanie gave me you and Dad. She did the right thing. I've always thought so. And I've never felt like I didn't have enough love. I've got you and I've got Dad and Grandma and Grandpa. That's more family than a lot of people have. But I'm glad that I'll get the chance to actually see her. Hug her." Marjorie smiled. "I'm not missing anything, though. My life is already complete."

That meant more to Ellie than maybe it should. She looked at Clark, and he smiled at her. Sixteen years together, and he was still her very favorite view on the planet. Her rock. The love of her life. The father of all five of their children. He still made her heart flutter.

They walked into the restaurant and were ushered into the private room.

Melanie and Ty were already sitting there. Ty looked so much more like Clark than he had for years. He'd put on muscle, weight, in the eighteen months since they'd quit using. And then there was Melanie. Her red hair was brushed and clean, her eyes bright with the kind of life that Ellie hadn't seen in them since they were in high school.

She and Clark had come together so many times to bail out Ty and Melanie. But there had never been a moment like this. Like this reunion.

Melanie's eyes filled with tears as she looked at Marjorie, who had red hair just like her own. "You're just beautiful," she said.

Marjorie smiled and stepped forward, hugging Melanie with an ease that surprised Ellie. Marjorie was an extroverted, confident teenage girl, but still, hugging a relative stranger was a big move.

"Thanks for my life," she said.

She stepped back and looked at Ellie.

Yeah. This life was pretty amazing. In that moment, Ellie felt entirely grateful for it too.

Grateful for everything.

They ate dinner and exchanged contact information, making plans to meet up again.

Ty and Melanie were working as addiction recovery counselors in Eugene. The two of them lived hours away, but they could all get together around the holidays, which suited Ellie.

When they got back home, Clark pulled her in for a hug. "You okay?"

"I'm good."

"It doesn't bother you at all, letting them have a relationship with Margie?"

"It really doesn't. Because they're part of the story, Clark. Our story."

He nodded. "That is true."

He brought her in for another hug and kissed her. It started out as a soft, supportive kiss, and then shifted to something else.

A chorus of howls broke up the kiss, and they looked at their five kids, who had come into the kitchen and were staring at them.

"You can't possibly still be hungry," he said. "You all ate."

That wasn't strictly true. Their youngest had not eaten. He had moved two meatballs around on a plate. Which was what he always did now.

"What we didn't expect was to find you making out in the kitchen," said Daniel, their fourteen-year-old.

"It's gross," agreed Ezekiel, who was twelve.

"It's love," Clark said. "You have so much of it around you all the time, you take it for granted. Varmints."

And with that he wrapped his arm around Ellie's neck and kissed her again.

And all she could think about was that they really had done it right.

Their kids were surrounded by an overflow of love, and there was more love to be had as they forged new relationships with Ty and Melanie.

She and Clark had a lot. But what they had most of was love.

That was a beautiful thing.

Please read on for excerpts from the authors' upcoming full-length novels!

The Lake House

Lori Foster

CHAPTER 1

Brogan Rafferty had a vague idea of how life should be. He hadn't ever lived it, but in his mind a picturesque image always formed: family, a small cozy home, people working together in love and loyalty . . . an ephemeral dream he'd never been able to grasp. He'd given up wanting it a long time ago.

But now, everything was different.

As he drove through Bramble, Kentucky, the old image materialized. Granted, the sun had just set and a rose hue bathed the houses, streets, and even the numerous trees, making everything prettier than it might otherwise be.

What really struck him was the quiet. There were no shouts, no sirens, nothing breaking—or blowing up. The few people he saw—walking together or sitting on porches—spoke quietly while smiling.

Driving slowly, he made note of the old-fashioned houses with vividly painted trim and bright front doors, lights shining from the windows. Unlike the settings familiar to him, no two houses were the same. The styles, sizes, and colors all varied.

Porch swings and window boxes filled with spring flowers

were a popular theme. Birds and squirrels played in massive trees. Brogan came to a stop when a deer bolted out in front of him, froze, then leaped away to disappear into the foliage. Wildlife was always a good sign of peace and tranquility. "This is the right place for us, Sugar. I can feel it."

From the back seat, the baby made sucking noises as she feasted on her fist. Hopefully, he'd find the right address soon. She needed to be fed, and probably needed a fresh diaper too.

Of all the things he'd survived in his lifetime—first as an emancipated youth living on his own, later getting through BUD/S and all the specialized training that followed, and then barely surviving an ambush and life-threatening injuries in the mountains of Afghanistan—caring for his tiny, precious cargo was the most challenging, and by far the most rewarding.

The mid-May weather was pleasantly warm, and spring rains had turned the grass and trees a lush green. Wildflowers grew in patches along the wooded side of the road, and occasionally on the other side, where he noted a few houses.

The farther he drove, the fewer houses he saw and the more natural the landscape became, until the road ended in a T and he had to choose left or right. Shortly after turning, he located the lake house.

The sight of the tiny place, set near the water and well tended, immediately warmed him. The glow of the sunset reflected over the rippling surface of the lake. All around them, flickering fireflies began to appear. Only a few at first, then more and more.

Who knew something as simple as fireflies could envelop him in a sense of rightness? He wasn't a man to indulge indecision. He evaluated, planned, and then acted. The fact that he was now responsible for such a vulnerable little life had made everything different. These days he constantly second-guessed himself, but this, the decision to come here, the plans he'd put into place, they were right. They had to be.

This was the perfect starting point for a new and better life.

He would not fail.

Gravel crunched as he pulled his black SUV into the driveway next to an older pale-blue minivan. The baby was fussing in earnest now. Brogan would rather listen to his own bones breaking than hear that tiny baby girl cry. Nothing shredded his heart the way she did.

After hurriedly parking, he rushed to the back door, opened it, and reached for her. Getting her out of the car seat took him a moment, and then he had to grab up the diaper bag.

She was soaking wet, which meant his shirt was now soaked too.

Fortunately, it was a warm evening, though he wasn't sure if it'd be too cool for a baby with a wet bottom.

"Shh, easy now, Sugar. I got ya." Thank God he had a bottle ready to go. One-armed, he opened the back of the SUV, shook out a blanket, and settled her on her back. "Gotta get ya dry first."

"Excuse me," came a soft, quiet voice.

Brogan glanced up and spotted a slim blonde on the walkway. Keeping his palm on the baby's belly so she couldn't roll, he slowly straightened.

Pixie Nolan. Yes, he was here to see her—it was the main reason Bramble had seemed fated to be his new home. He'd thought to have a day or two, perhaps a week to figure out how he wanted to approach her.

Time to improvise.

Her gaze went over him, and when she looked up again, her blue eyes were comically wide. "You're Mr. Rafferty?"

"Yes, ma'am. Cort Easton is expecting me."

Though she continued to stare, her smile was shy and sweet. "Cort is also my landlord. His flight plans changed, and he and his wife had to leave a day early for a vacation. He asked me to give you the keys when you arrived."

Unexpected, but still, he could handle it. "Thank you."

"I, um . . ." She laughed at herself. "Sorry, I don't mean to gawk, but you're really tall."

True, enough. At six-foot-five, he stood above many people. "Might seem so with you being so . . ." Calling her short might be insulting, so he substituted, "Petite." She couldn't be more than a few inches over five feet, with a delicate build that made it difficult to believe she was a mother.

"I'm Pixie Nolan."

He knew that already because he'd seen a small black-and-white photo that hadn't done her justice. "Nice to meet you." When the baby gave a piercing cry, he said, "And this noisy bundle is Shayna Raye. If you'll excuse me, I need to tend to her before she wakes up the entire town."

Pixie stood there, illuminated by the moon and the golden glow of a porch light. Her nearness caused an unusual restriction in his chest that limited his airflow as if he'd just taken a blast of artillery fire, feeling like that odd suspended moment in time before a man realized he'd been hit.

It was the anticipation, he decided.

So much hinged on building an association with her. It was what the baby deserved, what was expected, and yet it was something he'd never had.

Sucked that he knew almost nothing about blood families. All he knew was brotherhood. Hopefully, that would be enough.

Her brows came together in a puzzled frown. "You have a baby?"

A rhetorical question, obviously. "I've got my hands full here, so my attention is needed. I've got the hang of diaper changes, but not so much in the back of my SUV."

She inched closer and peeked around him. "Oh, yes." With a light laugh, she said, "I've been there, done that, so I understand. Here, let me help." She moved to the other side of him and retrieved a diaper from the bag, effortlessly opening it. "I'll hold the bottle if you want to handle the rest."

Damn, but he could smell her, a light scent of flowers and sunshine and possibly baby powder. The restriction in his chest increased. "You think it's too cool out here in the night air for me to swap out her clothes?"

"It's a warm night, so she'd be fine, but would you rather change her inside?" She nodded at his shirt. "You're already wet."

"True enough." As he spoke, Shayna decided to wail again. "It was a long drive and she's getting fussy."

"Long drives make me cranky too," she said, and then, "I didn't realize you had a daughter. Cort only mentioned one person."

"Is it a problem?"

"No, of course not."

"I'm glad to hear it." Carefully, Brogan gathered up the baby, settling her against his chest and getting the bottle back in her mouth without her getting out a single additional wail. He felt triumphant.

"Good job," Pixie praised as she folded the wet blanket he'd used, wrapped up the sopping diaper, and grabbed the diaper bag. "Come on. I'll show you the house. You'll love it." As she led him to the front door, she said, "I lived here with my son until recently. Actually, I'd have been happy to stay here, but Andy is so active now, Cort insisted he needed more room. I'm in the guest cottage just up the street." She tipped her head to the left. "Over that way is where Cort and Marlow live. You'll like them. Everyone around here does."

A dozen questions came to Brogan, but he tamped down his curiosity. If he got too nosy, he might offend her. "You like to fish?"

She stepped into the house and moved aside. "No, but Cort does. Marlow and I just enjoy the sunrises and sunsets."

"Go boating or swimming?"

"Not much." As if confiding a secret, she said, "There are things in the water. Big fish. Occasionally a snake. Snapping turtles."

He couldn't hold back his grin. "Nothing that would hurt you."

"Trust me, I've heard it all, but I still choose to stay out of the deeper water. My son and I sometimes sit in the shallow water at the sandy beach area where he can play, though of course I can't take my eyes off him."

"Where's your son now?" For many reasons, Brogan was interested in meeting the boy. Pixie didn't know it, but it was because of her son that he was here.

"It's close to his bedtime, so he's with a friend." Again confiding in him, she said, "When I came here a year ago, everyone welcomed me. Even better, they all fell in love with Andy. I'm never short of babysitters when I need one, though I don't like to leave him very often."

Was that a hint? "Guess I'm holding you up." He should have realized. "If you want me to sign something, show some ID, we can take care of that real fast so you can get home."

"No, it's fine." She smiled at Shayna. "Babies first, right?" Walking again, she said, "This is the sitting room; down that hall is the single bedroom and a bathroom. Everything you need is already there. Blankets, pillows, towels. Even soap and shampoo, though you probably have your own."

He had a small overnight kit with a toothbrush and toothpaste, shaving gear, and soap. Toiletries were not, and never had been, his priority.

"I have the paperwork here in the kitchen."

Everything about the place was miniature. Small rooms, small furniture, and a kitchen that was no more than a single row of cabinets over a sink and stove, with a narrow pantry and apartment-sized refrigerator. Good thing he was used to living lean.

The chairs at the two-seater corner table didn't look sturdy enough to support a man of his size.

Pixie either didn't notice his scrutiny or assumed he'd love the place as much as she claimed to. And honestly, it didn't matter. He needed a safe, clean space for the baby. Nothing more.

She was his priority. Her comfort and security mattered more than anything else.

"There's a stack washer-dryer in the utility closet." She looked around as if seeing the tiny house for the first time. "I know it's a tight space, but when I lived here, it just meant less to keep up with. Babies, as I'm sure you know, require the lion's share of your attention."

Brogan leaned back on the counter, set the empty bottle in the sink, and put Shayna to his shoulder so he could burp her. While he gently rubbed her back in a circular motion, he agreed with her assessment. "Logic doesn't apply, right? You'd think a tiny person with a smaller appetite, wearing only itty-bitty clothes and sleeping most of the time, would require less care, but somehow it's the opposite." His little angel belched, squirmed a moment, and then got comfortable in the crook of his neck.

Christ, he loved her, more than he'd known was possible.

"Around-the-clock care," Pixie said softly.

"Not that I'm complaining." Never. Having the baby's care entrusted to him was the greatest gift he'd ever received in his entire life. "It's fascinating, though."

When Pixie grinned, he didn't just see it, he felt it, clear down to his soul. Not even to himself did he want to sound corny, but she was like sunshine breaking through darkness. The magic of laughter after hearing so many broken cries.

She didn't know it, but she was an open door when every other exit was blocked.

He hoped she'd be okay with his plans. Everything he'd read about her made it seem possible.

"You might want to get her out of those wet clothes before she falls asleep again. You don't want to deal with diaper rash."

Of course, Pixie didn't know that she'd just stepped on a topic about as explosive as a landmine. He breathed a little harder, remembering things better left forgotten. He had Shayna now and he was determined she'd never suffer another ill.

Getting his mouth to smile wasn't easy, but he forced it, adding a lighthearted truth. "This girl sleeps like a champ. I've changed her, and once even bathed her, while she dozed through it."

"It's amazing how trusting babies can be."

It was especially incredible that this baby, after what she'd been through, could trust him—but she did. His voice emerged as a rasp. "When they're feeling secure. When they have reason to trust."

She tipped her head, studying him curiously. "As all babies should."

Glad that she shared that sentiment, he nodded. "Hundred percent."

"Do you have a crib for her in your car?"

"A Moses basket, though I'll probably need to get her a crib soon. She's started rolling over, and once she starts, she wants to keep going."

With a quiet laugh, Pixie asked, "Clean baby blankets? Another bottle ready?"

It amused him to see her shift into mom mode. He could take exception to her question, which suggested he couldn't handle things, but obviously she loved kids and knew what she was doing. "Got all that," he said. "Though I'll prepare a few more bottles tonight." Worries caught up to him and he admitted in a low voice, "Sometimes she'll almost sleep through the night, like five hours or so, and it scares me. I almost preferred it when she was up every couple of hours." It gave him the chance to hold her, to know she was okay. To tell her over and over that he'd never let her down, would never leave her alone, that he'd protect her always.

Reaching out, Pixie brushed the back of one finger over Shayna's silky hair. "No other kids?"

He shook his head. "I wasn't here for her until she was nearly two months old." Remembering felt like having a part of his guts removed—without anesthesia. "I'm military and I was away. . . ." *Dying*. Or at least that was what he'd wanted at the time.

To be left alone to quietly die. To join his brothers. To escape the gnawing guilt of surviving—when they hadn't.

Then he'd gotten the news about a half sister he barely knew, the niece he'd never met, and God, how it had invigorated him with purpose. He had a reason to go on. One hell of a reason.

"Cort was military too," she shared. "A marine recon sniper. He's considered a hometown hero around here."

"Once a marine, always a marine," Brogan replied. He felt the same way. The military was now in his blood, the better part of him, the survival instinct that kept him going—and thank God it had, since Shayna needed him now. "As a SEAL, I had the honor of working with a few of those guys."

"You're a SEAL?" Awe sounded in her voice.

Damn it, why had he said that? He *never* talked about his service. She'd taken him by surprise, just tossing out Cort's rank like that. She and Cort must be close for him to have shared it with her. Instead of answering her question, Brogan changed the subject. "What do you need me to sign?"

Pixie immediately got the hint. She took a seat at the table and turned the paper toward him. "Cort said you already sent the down payment and first month's rent, so all I need is your ID, and then if you'll sign here, I'll give you the basic rundown and leave you with the keys."

Brogan knew he'd chased her off, but he'd tackle that issue another time. Right now, he needed to unload the car and get Shayna settled.

He held the baby close and withdrew his driver's license from his wallet.

Pixie was quick to confirm his ID. After he'd signed the paper and she'd put it in her purse, she sent a worried glance toward the baby. "Do you need help bringing a few things inside?"

"I've got it, thanks."

"You're sure? I wouldn't mind. . . ."

She had her face turned up to his while she nervously twirled two fingers in her long pale hair. Damn, he wanted to spill his guts, to tell her the important role she could play in Shayna's life. Now was definitely not the time, though, not if he wanted full success. "I appreciate the offer, Pixie. Really, thank you. Right now, I think I just want to get my bearings."

Still, she hesitated.

He smiled. "I promise, we'll be fine for tonight. How about tomorrow you stop by and give me that rundown, maybe tell me a little about the town and where to find what?"

Nodding, she said, "Sure. Will noon work?" Without waiting for his agreement, she said, "Emergency numbers are on the fridge. I'm going to add my number real quick, just in case something comes up." Using the pen she'd given him to sign the four-month agreement, she jotted a number at the bottom of a long list that included police, fire department, hospital, and food delivery. As she hurriedly turned away to head for the door, she said, "Remote is with the TV. Outside lights are automatic dusk to dawn. Hot water doesn't last too long, which is something I found out the hard way, so you might want to shower before doing any laundry. Oh, and Cort likes to make sure the basics are already in the kitchen cupboards, and some necessities are in the fridge. If you need anything else before noon tomorrow, just let me know."

After saying all that, she practically clamped her mouth shut and rushed off as if being chased.

In case he'd somehow made her uncomfortable, he trailed more slowly behind her. The last thing he wanted from her was wariness.

"See you tomorrow," he said, as she all but jogged to her van.

With a careless wave, she got in the vehicle and left.

Brogan stood there with the baby in his arms and watched as her headlights went down the road, then turned into another driveway. She was nearby, yet there was some property between them. A nice arrangement.

Presumptuous as it might be, he already imagined Pixie in their future, his and Shayna's. She had a good heart; that much was clear. She wouldn't deny them.

The only problem might be Cort. Pixie was obviously close to the man. Because Cort had a military background, he was bound to be protective. That meant he wouldn't like Brogan's plans.

The baby stirred, rubbing her button nose against his shirt, stretching a bit, then settling in again. He decided he'd deal with the issue of Cort when it became necessary. He wouldn't let anything stand in his way.

"Now," Brogan said, his palm moving up and down the baby's narrow back. "It's time for you, Sugar—and our fresh start." He brushed his mouth over her downy crown, inhaled her sweet, comforting scent, and headed back inside.

It was time to get started.

Christmas Valley

Maisey Yates

Redemption is for men who care. I lost all that a long time ago.
—Butch Hancock's Diary, June 15, 1867

Cassidy Wilder had known exactly what she wanted since she was nine years old. To have in this order: a home of her own, a place in the town of Rustler Mountain, and to marry Dalton Wade.

She now had a small home on her brother's ranch—not quite what she was after, but something adjacent. Her brother Austin had turned the tide of public opinion on the reputation of their outlaw family over the last couple of years—which again, wasn't her doing but had given her a sense of belonging she'd been missing.

So really all that was left was marrying Dalton.

The issue was that she might die a vestal virgin waiting for him to ever kiss her.

Dalton was her brother Flynn's best friend, and she knew he was being respectful by not making a move on her. He was being a good friend, a good . . . well, whatever he was to her. Because he was a good guy, and he probably had that weird, wrongheaded idea that sex would corrupt her.

Well, she wouldn't say no to some corruption, but it was becoming clearer and clearer to her that she was going to have to make the first move.

And what better time than now? This season.

The season.

Fa-la-la-la fuck me please, cowboy.

That little internal thought made her shiver, just slightly. Whether because she was pondering the meaning of the word, or because she was afraid she'd be struck by a falling Christmas tree for being so irreverent around a holy season, she wasn't sure.

But the season was upon them, nonetheless.

Rustler Mountain was definitely beginning to look like winter was approaching. The trees in front of the town hall had all turned a vibrant red and orange, and Cassidy knew that meant the leaves would wither and drop by next week. The color was vivid, but fleeting, a metaphor, probably, for something she had never experienced.

Every weekend between now and Christmas, there would be festivities on the main street of town. While Cassidy didn't like to betray the fact that she was secretly soft, in her own heart she could admit it. She loved the decorations, the music, the food. Sometimes she thought that if she could immerse herself in Rustler Mountain Christmas, then she would forget all the Christmases that came before, and most crucially, the Christmas when her mother left her stranded on Austin's doorstep, making her a Christmas foundling at the mercy of three older half brothers who had never even known of her existence.

It would not be surprising if she hated Christmas. For a while it had been difficult. But Christmas in Florida had been different. The way the seasons changed—and they did change, contrary to what people who didn't live there believed—was different from the way they changed in Oregon. The air tasted different, the foliage behaved in a different manner. The way fall turned things crisp before winter made the landscape an easily shattered pane of ice was something she had never experienced until she moved here. Christmas had become a new tradition that had new meaning.

Now it reminded her of how lucky she was to have her older brothers. How lucky she was to have this place to call home. And really, how lucky she was to have Dalton. Her entire family was helping with her future sister-in-law's booth. Jessie Jane was doing blacksmithing demonstrations in a station by the courthouse and answering people's questions and concerns as Rustler Mountain's future mayor. Her term would begin in January.

Cassidy was walking toward the booth now, hands in her pockets, a scarf wrapped tightly around her neck to keep the chill at bay. She could hear music, laughter, conversation, could smell cinnamon, apples, and cloves on the air.

There were carolers walking toward her, wearing Victorian costumes, the men in top hats, the women in dark, high-collared dresses with bustled skirts. It was a familiar scene, and yet always different. Always a spectacle.

She quickened her pace as she moved toward the family booth, crossing the street while traffic stopped for her. She waved cheerily at the cars and kept on going.

There was a crowd around Jessie's booth, so she could barely see what was happening, though she could see sparks flying upward and people clapping.

She could see Austin, wearing a black cowboy hat, holding his daughter. And his wife, Millie, standing beside him holding his arm. The sight made Cassidy ache, but not in a bad way.

One of the things that Cassidy was having a difficult time wrapping her head around was how different everything was this Christmas.

A couple of years ago Austin and Millie had gotten married; then they had a baby. Then Carson married his best friend, Perry, and now Flynn and Jessie Jane were engaged after what seemed to Cassidy to be whirlwind fling.

She couldn't imagine anything like that.

Because Dalton wasn't a whirlwind.

He was stable and steady. He was everything she valued.

Right. All of the women he'd had casual affairs with would call him stable and steady.

Okay. Maybe they wouldn't.

But she knew him as stable and steady. He was always good to her. Always patient and wonderful and exceptionally kind.

He was everything she could ever want in a man.

The crowd around the booth began to disperse, and that was when she saw him.

Hands moving in broad gestures as he told a story that made Jessie and Perry double over with laughter. Cassidy felt an absurd prick of jealousy. She had nothing to be jealous about. Perry and Jessie weren't single.

She picked up her pace. She cut across the lawn rather than walking around the perimeter and ignored the delicious-smelling treats as she made a beeline for her family.

"Hi," she said.

The conversation broke off, and she became very aware of the fact that she had just crashed in. Not only that, but they had all responded to her appearance by ceasing their conversation.

Her brothers were careful with her. Maybe a little bit too careful, because of the circumstances surrounding her coming to Rustler Mountain. Everyone was so painfully aware of the fact that she'd been abandoned, and while it was really sweet that they worried about her and all, she didn't need to be treated like a charity case. Or like she was tragic.

Though, to be fair, she definitely acted like the youngest, most coddled member of the group. It was a learned habit. And now that everybody was pairing off, getting married, having children, it seemed . . . silly. She felt silly. She wanted things to change.

She looked at Dalton, and her heart jumped. "What's so funny?"

"Oh, I was talking about the time my brother and I were hunting and he got a deer. Then we came up over the mountain, and there was a bear feeding on the deer that he just dropped. Well, then he got the bear, and went running down the hill shouting 'Two for one!' "

She knew this story. Of course she did. It had happened way back when Dalton was a kid, and he got a lot of mileage out of it. But she laughed anyway, because she loved to hear him tell it.

"That's ridiculous," Jessie said, wiping a tear underneath her eye. "What are the chances?"

"They must not be very good, because I've never known another person that it happened to. And it never happened to him again."

"He was just lucky I guess," Cassidy said, smiling at him.

"I guess so," he responded. "I know I am."

And she tried to pick that apart. To see if there was anything underlying those words. A secret message that was meant only for her. Or something.

Jessie sighed heavily and looked at her phone. "I have to start another round again. Just pounding out a shoe, but look, there's a crowd coming."

"You look tired," Cassidy said, meaning to be helpful.

But Jessie flinched. "Do I?"

"Not in a bad way," Cassidy said hurriedly. "In a way that suggests you're very industrious."

Her older brother Flynn reached over and clapped his hand on her shoulder. "Quit while you're only a little bit behind, Cass."

Cassidy felt her smile falter. "Can I help with anything?"

"You can go gather some people," Jessie said.

"I will," she said, scampering away and finding a knot of teenagers. "There's a blacksmithing demonstration starting over there. Free to watch."

She moved through the group of people, marveling at all the strange faces. So many people drove all the way out to Rustler Mountain around the holidays. It was a local tourist attraction. The kind of place that was worth an hour's drive.

Sometimes Cassidy wondered what it would be like to live

close to a movie theater, a chain restaurant, or a Walmart, instead of being well over an hour away. But her ultimate conclusion was that it just wasn't the life for her.

She liked living here. The sense of community, the traditions.

She had no intention of leaving. She liked stability. The familiarity of Rustler Mountain. The sameness of life here.

Well, a lot of things in her life had changed lately, but *she* had no intention of changing.

Except, she did want things to change with Dalton. It was what she had always hoped for.

And if he rejects you, then what?

No. She'd had enough bad things happen to her. She had been over this in her mind before. If you were abandoned by your mother, brought to a town you had never even heard of to live with your father, who died right before you arrived, leaving you totally stranded with three feral older brothers, then you were owed some smooth sailing.

She was convinced of that. Or rather, she wanted to be convinced of that.

She gathered quite a crowd to visit the booth, where she watched her brother admiring Jessie's handiwork.

"She's something," said Flynn.

The way he looked at his fiancée, it was just so obvious he was head over heels in love. It was really something. It brought her back to that earlier interaction with Dalton. What had she seen in his eyes?

She couldn't be sure.

But then, nothing ventured nothing gained.

She turned her focus on Jessie, who was heating the horseshoe, bringing it out of the forge when it was bright red, and hammering it forcefully, the sound of metal on metal filling the air.

She went on until the shoe was the perfect shape, then doused it in water, cooling it. She gave it to a triumphant little girl in the front row.

"I didn't know girls could do jobs like that," the little girl said.

"Of course we can," said Jessie. "And I'm also going to be the mayor of this town. We can do anything we put our minds to."

Cassidy smiled. Because the exchange was adorable. And honestly, it just made her proud to call Jessie part of the family. Funny, because Jessie was a Hancock, and only two years ago, her older brother Austin would have had a heart attack if he'd been told that a Hancock was going to marry into his family.

Wilder family lore was deep and vast. Well, the lore of this entire town was like that. Founded during the gold rush, Rustler Mountain had been filled with pioneers, both good and bad. When Austin had started doing deep historical research into their family roots, it turned out that the ones who had been touted as heroic for years were somewhat more complex.

For years town lore had been all about the heroes and the villains. The outlaws and the lawmen. And of course, the Wilder family had been among the outlaws.

Her brother was named after Austin Wilder, who had been a stagecoach and train robber, notorious throughout the state of Oregon for his crimes. He had ridden with his two brothers and a fourth gang member named Butch Hancock. Until Lee Talbot, sheriff of Rustler Mountain, had shot Austin Wilder dead in the street and had the other Wilders hanged for suspicion of murder.

But it turned out that Lee Talbot had colluded with Butch Hancock, agreeing to give him immunity if the sheriff could have the notoriety of taking down Oregon's most notorious gang. The Wilders had been criminals, but they had never committed murder.

Austin had set the record straight in his best-selling book, and Millie had started setting the record straight throughout town, which had led to a lot of historical inaccuracies and half-truths being corrected. Now the true history of the town could be told, not just by the victors—white men who liked to claim ultimate authority—but through the stories of Chinese immigrants, of Black settlers who had met with hostility and been kept out of the state because of virulently racist laws, and of course, those of the Native tribes whose land had been taken from them.

So maybe things did change. And some of them definitely needed to.

She looked over at Dalton.

And then the atmosphere around the booth changed. Shifted. As if the air itself shivered.

She turned because she was compelled, like steel to a magnet. And not just her apparently, because every head turned.

West Hancock had just arrived. He wasn't dressed seasonally.

He wore a tight black T-shirt, muscular arms on display for no reason. Black inked licked up his forearms, past his biceps, and disappeared beneath the sleeves of the shirt.

He also had on a black cowboy hat, black jeans, black boots.

He was, without a doubt, the only man in town with a more dangerous reputation than her brothers.

If the Wilders were outlaws, the Hancocks were the outlaws the outlaws didn't associate with.